THE LOST TRAIL

THE LOST TRAIL

Lauran Paine

This Large Print book is published by BBC Audiobooks Ltd, Bath, England and by Thorndike Press®, Waterville, Maine, USA.

Published in 2004 in the U.K. by arrangement with Golden West Literary Agency.

Published in 2004 in the U.S. by arrangement with Golden West Literary Agency.

U.K. Hardcover ISBN 1–4056–3073–6 (Chivers Large Print)
U.K. Softcover ISBN 1–4056–3074–4 (Camden Large Print)
U.S. Softcover   ISBN 0–7862–6827–1 (Nightingale)

The text of this Large Print edition is unabridged.
Other aspects of the book may vary from the original edition.

Set in 16 pt. New Times Roman.

Printed in Great Britain on acid-free paper.

British Library Cataloguing in Publication Data available

Library of Congress Control Number: 2004107028

CHAPTER ONE

MORGAN VALLEY

The people who had originally settled in Morgan Valley had arrived in their prairie schooners from Pennsylvania. The second wave of westerning argonauts who had arrived, and who for the most part had pressed on to Oregon and upper California, had come from Missouri, and although the root-stock had been fundamentally the same a century and more earlier, by the time each group was prepared to emigrate west of the Missouri River into the lawless, raw wilderness the differences which had divided a nation, brought it to the bloodiest conflict of its history, and had settled some issues such as U.S. slavery, had also ingrained in these people all the sentiments and convictions which would keep them separate for another century yet to come.

Missouri had been a slave-state. Pennsylvania had been a free-state. Four years of a battle a day resulting in the total exhaustion of Missouri and the Confederacy, and almost total exhaustion for Pennsylvania and the Federal Union, brought victory to the Union and a degree of deep and abiding bitterness to the losers including Missourians.

1

Twelve years later, after the last fusillade, the last drum-roll, the final furling and casing of the colours, the Union's blue-bellies had gone headlong into a stunning disaster on the Little Big Horn, miles west of civilisation, and miles north of the Morgan Valley settlement. An officer named Custer whose doggedly loyal wife Elizabeth had few tears left to shed, led his troops with a flourish and a blare of bugles right straight down through the gauntlet of death.

What made it so hard to accept was that the nation was no longer small nor weak, and the harassed tribesmen had been losing battles steadily year in and year out until their demoralisation had left them hopelessly divided and vulnerable.

It was impossible. Army generals in Washington knew absolutely that it could not happen. The triumphant Federal Union had emerged from the Civil War battle-tested and war-tempered. It could not be defeated on the Continent, nor had it ever been defeated, and certainly not by Indians.

No one expected the desperate and embattled tribesmen to amass. There were more than five thousand fighting Indians strung out up and down the Little Big Horn, over next to the river, up and along the grassy hills and ridges, and down through the glades and vales. The army rode to conquer with a handful of troops and was engulfed by the largest congregation of redskins ever known to have assembled.

In Washington, the electrifying news was at first disbelieved, then accepted with recriminations. Across the land people were outraged. In Morgan Valley the Missourians said flat-out that Yankees had never understood Indians, had never known how to handle them, and this was exactly what they deserved. In fact, a few people were pleased, but they were the radicals, the out-and-out die-hard Confederates—called Secesh, for Secessionists. Generally, even though the Missourians lay all the blame on the blue-belly army—the same army which had defeated them twelve years earlier—they did not go as far as to say Custer and his martyrs had it coming. No matter how much bitterness might still rankle, deep down, most people disapproved of what had occurred on the Little Big Horn.

All that summer there were arguments, even a few fights but nothing serious, and by autumn it was no longer Custer—if it really ever had been—who was at the bottom of the antagonistic divergencies, it was the same old resentment which had flourished for years before Custer rode out of Fort Lincoln heading for immortality along the Little Big Horn. It was Yankee-Pennsylvanians and Confederate-Missourians. Loyalists versus Rebels.

The way Doctor Hubert Spence put it was

3

succinct enough. 'If the 7th and Custer had whipped hell out of Two Moons, Rain-In-The-Face, Gall and all the rest of them the Secesh would have accused the army of bullying its Indians. As it was, the warwhoops whipped the army, so the Missourians say the army had it coming. The only way the Secesh would have approved of anything at all that happened up there would have been if it had been Robert E. Lee or Longstreet, or maybe even old Jeff Davis himself, leading the troops, and they had trounced the redskins.'

Missouri tempers, unreliable at best, heard this statement repeated often enough—but Bert Spence was the only physician and surgeon within a week's ride of Morgan Valley—so except for a little muttering and a few hostile glares, the doctor survived quite well.

It helped too, that Doctor Hubert Spence had been a surgeon in the Confederate Army. The other Secesh said he was a traitor for saying bad things about the Missourians, but the Yankee-Pennsylvanians just smiled.

Dan Cowper who was the undertaker and proprietor of the local apothecary shop, with a sabre scar down from the hairline along his left cheek, in the form of a red crescent, made the best neutral comment when he said, 'Doc Spence hit the nail plumb on the head. I got scars on me from Jeb Stuart's Confederate cavalry, and I got other reason to hate the

4

Secesh, but that's over and long past, and Custer is an excuse not a reason. Our trouble here in Morgan Valley is ourselves, nothing more and nothing less. A bunch of bigots live here, but Doc Spence isn't one of them.'

Dan Herlihy who owned and operated the *Buffalo Saloon* in Morganton, the Irish-born son of emigrants who had half-matured around Boston and who had come west after the death of his wife and baby daughter in an apartment-house fire in Massachusetts, was greying, big, burly and blue-eyed, and eloquently opinionated. Like many Irishmen, even those born and reared thousands of miles from the Auld Sod, Dan Herlihy could be relied upon to take a stand. He did it the autumn of the Custer affair by saying there was no finer army on earth than the Federal Union's blue brigades, over half of which were Irish; it was those glory-hunting officers like George Custer who brought shame and disaster every time, not the enlisted men.

Dan had been a Yankee infantryman, otherwise when Waite Culpepper the rangeboss of Hardin's Ox-Yoke cow outfit stood at the bar in Herlihy's place and said the reason Custer had got wiped out was because blue-belly soldiers couldn't fight, Dan probably would not have launched himself over the top of his bar.

That fight was something the spectators vowed they would never forget. Waite

5

Culpepper was rangy and tough and younger, and he too had been an infantryman, but on the Rebel side.

They had almost demolished the windows, the tables and chairs, even the roadway doors before Dan had caught Waite coming in and had almost torn his head loose with an uppercut which had everything in it desperate Dan Herlihy still possessed.

It took a solid hour to bring Waite Culpepper around, and he did not appear in Morganton again for two weeks. Rumour starting at Ox-Yoke had it that Waite could not recall things for several days after that fight. His memory, or something in his head anyway, had been damaged. Gradually though he recovered.

Colonel George Hardin rode into town two days after that memorable engagement, tied up out front of Constable Will Chance's jailhouse-office and went stonily to meet Will without allowing the younger and larger man to get a word in edgeways. Colonel Hardin had summed it up for Will in one fierce sentence. 'The next time I'll come in with the whole crew, armed, and we'll settle this gawddamned Secesh-Yankee business once and for all.'

Will listened without opening his mouth, and after iron-eyed Colonel Hardin had ridden back out of town, with his rangerider-escort, Constable Chance went down to Rex Morgan's shoeing shop and buggy works to say that he was no longer going to be able to look the other way when the menfolk around town took it into their heads to fight.

Reg, the last—and only—descendant of Elias Morgan who had founded the valley and Morganton as a social and economic unit, was burly and taciturn with grey eyes and a square jaw. Like Will Chance, Reg had not been in the Civil War. He said, 'It's springtime again, Will. Everyone blames all the activity on the Yanks or the Secesh—hell—it's springtime and the sap is running again, that's all . . . Custer? Just another vain, stupid son of a bitch. It's not him that's got things going anyway; the sap is running like it does every springtime.'

'All the same from now on,' stated Will, leaning and watching Reg at work on a wagon tyre, 'It's got to stop. Old Colonel Hardin's roiled up.'

Reg was indifferent about that also. 'He's always roiled up. Ever since I can remember he's been roiled up. My paw used to say Old Hardin's just hangin' on and waitin' and hopin' for all he's worth the South will rise again. He's never got over being a colonel and bein' able to order folks around.'

Hardin was indeed a harsh and commanding individual but it was not fair to say he wanted things back the way they had been. He owned one of the largest cow outfits in Morgan Valley. He was no has-been grieving over a past which had reflected upon him with

7

glory. He was a successful cowman *and* a former Confederate colonel.

He was one of the few Secesh in Morgan Valley the Missourians were mute about. He was one of them, and in fact he had been an exalted one of them, but he happened to also be a very difficult man at times; it did not matter to Colonel Hardin whether a loafer on his range was a Yank or a Rebel, if he did not work and work very hard the colonel would, first of all, tongue-lash him within an inch of his life, then the colonel would fire him.

Hardin had once made an unforgivable remark about the Missourians. 'If ignorance is ever to triumph out here there will be Missourians in the van of it,' he had said after a particular wave of anti-Yankee feeling had swept through Morgan Valley.

The Missourians also feared Hardin. For that matter so did many of the Yankees. So did Constable Will Chance; he had been striving for several years to keep on the good side of the older man. He was still striving to do that, but Will Chance also had a limit just like everyone else.

Hardin's one comment about the Custer affair found no great favour with either faction in Morgan Valley, but Colonel Hardin had not said it with that in mind. He simply gave his personal opinion of a colonel who was also a brevet general, who would deliberately abandon his artillery and lead brave men to

8

their deaths simply because he had great personal—and political—aspirations.

'That son of a bitch should have been shot off his horse by his own officers before they allowed him to lead them into a place they knew damned well none of them would come out of alive.'

That kind of talk was neutral; it did not favour the Secesh or the Yanks, and the result was that neither the Secesh nor the Yanks liked it.

The trouble with telling the plain truth was just that it never did much for the cause of partisanship, and for that reason was never too popular.

CHAPTER TWO

MEN AND SEASONS

Morganton, like Morgan Valley, had been opened up by a gun-handy, heavy-handed Texan and his raw, fearless, hard-riding crew. The only Morgan left was Reg, who rarely mentioned his grandfather, or even his father, and yet he was like his grandfather in some ways. For example Reg Morgan was blunt and forthright when he had anything to say. If someone chose to take umbrage, that suited Reg just as much as it had suited old Elias, his grandfather.

The difference was that old Elias had been a hip-shooter, a man who made snap judgements and instant decisions. More often than not old Elias's judgement was sound, but there had been plenty of times when it hadn't been, and old Elias's major sin was that he would not, come hell or high water, admit to being wrong.

Reg on the other hand never made a quick judgement nor a rash decision. Sometimes in fact he waited so long he seemed to suffer from chronic procrastination.

There was another difference; old Elias had spoken up instantly on just about any subject. Reg was often taciturn, thoughtful to the point of doggedness, and unwilling to down-grade anyone. Elias Morgan had despised Indians and Mexicans, and had been suspicious and wary of anyone who had not originated in his native Texas.

Reg, like Constable Will Chance, had not been in the war—he'd been too young at the time—and although he had personal opinions about which had been the correct cause, he never took sides and bluntly castigated the older men who did. Furthermore, he held no grudge against Mexicans or Indians, but then his generation had never had the reasons to do this; at least they had never had the same kind of hair-curling reasons their parents and grandparents had had.

Once, when Colonel Hardin, who had fought them all, pepperbellies, warwhoops, renegades of both breeds as well as the bluebellies, made a slighting remark at Morgan's shoeing shed, Reg had straightened up, put down the foot of Hardin's black ridgling, and had said, 'Colonel; you believe what you like, but if it's got to do with folks you don't approve of—don't bring into my shop with you.'

Few people spoke up to George Hardin. That particular time the colonel hadn't said a word. He had stood looking at Reg Morgan stonily for a long while, then in silence he had departed from the shop.

Hardin was a widower, as was Doctor Spence, and when folks had occasion to discuss the colonel, as they frequently did since he was the largest and presumably wealthiest cowman in Morgan Valley, it was sometimes said that what George Hardin needed was a wife.

Dan Herlihy thought otherwise. 'I wouldn't wish that off on to a decent woman,' he maintained. 'What old Hardin needs is for someone to stomp down hard on him the very next time he acts arrogant.'

It never happened. Reg had spoken up to Hardin, and perhaps other men also had over the years, but the people around Morgan Valley who might do this were scarce.

Nor was George Hardin arrogant. Maybe in

Herlihy's opinion he was, but there was reason to question whether or not Herlihy really understood the meaning of the word. Dan was never without an opinion; he seemed to possess some inherent conviction that made it necessary for him to believe people should always have considered every issue they were likely to encounter, but his judgement was faulty upon occasion and his understanding of some of the issues he was perfectly willing to expound upon seemed vague at times.

When someone brought an old newspaper to the saloon from the stage-station across the road, and several bar-room patrons read a front-page article about Ladd Denton the notorious gunman being pardoned by the military governor of the Territory of New Mexico, Dan said it was a crying shame and a dirty outrage that just because an outlaw and renegade had once been an army officer he had been excused from breaking the law.

In fact the reason Ladd Denton had got that governor's pardon had been because Ladd Denton, at the risk of his life, had shot it out with Mexican border-jumpers who had been attacking a stranded stagecoach when Denton had loped up after hearing the gunfire.

Inside that stagecoach had been two nuns from an Albuquerque convent, a mother with two small daughters, and His Excellency the Military Governor.

Nor did Dan Herlihy read the article past its

first two paragraphs or he would have learned, also, that the pardon only extended to the present; if Ladd Denton broke the law in the future the pardon would be revoked and every allegation against him made before the pardon, would once more be in full effect.

And Ladd Denton had been a Union officer. Herlihy would never have opened his mouth if he had read down that far.

Still and all, Dan was a generous, understanding man. At times he was even sympathetic and compassionate.

In short, Herlihy was like everyone else; he was endowed with roughly an equal share of virtues and vices. It depended upon which of his moods predominated, and just like everyone else his moods varied and were usually unpredictable.

Doctor Spence was occasionally justly critical of Herlihy, but then Doc had lived a long while, had seen it all and had encountered all kinds, so he could perhaps be excused for his cynicism. This was not a delightful world and the inhabitants of it often smelled bad, acted worse, and throve on major or minor treachery.

Doc's reaction to Herlihy's comments upon the governor's pardon was one pithy comment made across Dan's bar within Herlihy's hearing.

'No man is consistently good nor consistently bad, and that includes bartenders and saloon owners, and I wonder if any of *them* would have ridden up single-handed to take on a band of Mex brigands!'

Colonel Hardin's rangeboss, who had plenty of reason to enjoy Dan Herlihy's discomfiture, grinned when Doc said that. So did a number of other patrons of the *Buffalo Saloon.*

Ladd Denton, though, was never more than a subject to be discussed. No one in Morganton—at least as far as they ever admitted—had ever met or even seen Ladd Denton. In the whole of Morgan Valley there had never been more than a handful of acknowledged outlaws, although it was rumoured almost every riding season that one of the outlying cattle ranches had a hired-on cowboy who was in fact a deadly renegade using his range skills and another name to avoid detection by the law. This was one of the oldest bits of gossip on every summertime cow range, and if it happened that a cowboy suddenly demonstrated that he was very fast with his sixgun and very deadly with it perhaps against a rattlesnake or a bear, the credibility was given a solid boost, but as a matter of fact professional outlaws although they may have originated as cowboys, very rarely reverted back to that avocation.

As for the good shots among the rangemen: There was little else for many riders to do, day in and day out when they were endlessly riding, than to practise with their guns. Many of them became very proficient, but they rarely became outlaws along with that proficiency.

Ladd Denton was more legend than man, to the people of Morgan Valley. Even Colonel Custer who was now dead, did not become a legend as quickly nor as enduringly as did Ladd Denton, who was still alive.

Like many legends, the stories surrounding the name of Denton accumulated too fast for one man to have taken part in all of them. Ladd Denton became the Robin Hood of every cow-camp. A few men like Doctor Spence who had known outlaws and who willingly and pithily put them into proper perspective, were not believed. People, Doc said, did not want their legends de-bunked, and he was correct, they didn't.

Morgan Valley had a few legends, mostly created around old Elias and those unkempt, unshorn, swaggering Texans he had arrived in the valley with, driving his first herd of slab-sided, wicked-horned, evil-dispositioned Longhorn cattle.

There were several legends about the Indians who had been here first and who had resisted old Elias and his riders. There were also rumours that the descendants of some of those old warwhoops were still skulking somewhere on the outskirts of the valley, perhaps in the foothills or the more distant, heat-blurred far-away mountains. No one went to see; no one really cared. If the Indians wanted the hills they were welcome to them, their conquerors and the descendants of those conquerors had the grassland, and that alone really mattered.

Will Chance, who had been a rangerider for eight years before hiring on as the town marshal of Morganton, usually heard the rumours of holdout-Indians first, and Will usually made a policy of never repeating those stories for a very basic reason. He did not want to have to go Indian-hunting in mountains which the warwhoops knew better than he did, and he secretly did not altogether approve of herding folks, Indians or any other kind of folks, on to reservations. As long as those holdouts did not make trouble and were discreet about stealing a few horses now and then, and were prudent in the butchering of an occasional beef for winter meat, Will could conveniently forget the stories people occasionally told him.

Waite Culpepper said Will was lazy. Dan Herlihy said he was not lazy, he just didn't believe in going round being obnoxious just because he wore that badge on his shirt.

Dan Cowper figured it had to be somewhere in between. He had seen Will loafing at the stage-station office a few times, and he had seen Will sitting relaxed in the shade down at the liverybarn swapping lies with the liveryman and some of his cronies. Dan's assessment was candid.

16

'Will's a good lawman for Morganton. He don't stir up any more trouble than the town can stand, and when he's not doing that, he's certainly entitled to ruminate if he's a mind to . . . When you're in my business—out back in the wagon-shed embalming one of 'em—you just naturally wonder why in hell any of us at all do all the things we do and go to all the efforts we go to.'

People as a rule did not mention Cowper's sideline of undertaking, and they had a wholesome respect for his learning as a druggist. There were a few folks around the valley who whispered about Dan being able to make potions in his back room that would simply do all sorts of near-magical things. But undertaking was something people without much of a life-expectancy rarely talked about.

The stage company's station-master from across the road, roughly opposite Dan's saloon where the corralyard and office stood, was a supporter of Will Chance because over the years Will had sedulously gone after highwaymen who had stopped coaches, and while Will had seldom brought back the loot, he had more often than not brought back at least a horse, or perhaps one of the dead highwaymen; a score like that earned respect in any corralyard.

As Henry Devereaux said, there had been extremely few lawmen in Morgan Valley since he had been there who had made as much of

17

an effort as Will Chance made, and on those grounds Henry had to take exception to Waite Culpepper's remark about Will being lazy.

An unnamed alcoholic who worked as hostler for the liveryman summed it up rather well. Over a drink at Dan's bar this nameless individual said, 'As long as people in a place like Morgan Valley have nothing worse to worry about than each other, things have got to be operating well and smoothly.'

That hostler had ridden a coach southward a week later and no one ever heard of him again. There were always floaters like that passing through, and some of them, like this one, were undoubtedly better educated than almost anyone else in town. Old Barleycorn was no respecter of castes at all.

That hostler's comment had been entirely true. As long as the people of Morgan Valley had nothing more critical to worry about than each other, and their old-time affiliations north or south of the Mason-Dixon Line, things were generally operating fairly smoothly.

The difficulty was, of course, that exactly as Doctor Spence had applied a loosely-worded natural law to human beings in Morgan Valley, by saying they were moody and unpredictable, the same natural law applied to events, to circumstances, to the ebb and flow which accompanied each end every springtime in Morgan Valley and everywhere else on earth.

CHAPTER THREE

ROUTINES AND AVERAGES

Devereaux's northbound coach out of Morganton heading for Chamberlain by way of Buckhorn Pass was held up seven miles north of town and seven miles south of the pass, or equal distance both ways, at a spot which had often been viewed as a likely place to effect a hold-up because there was a jumble of alien rocks as tall as mounted men on each side of the road.

There were no other rocks like those anywhere in Morgan Valley. This uniqueness had centuries earlier encouraged the superstitious tribesmen to endow those lichen-covered, scaly-looking old stones with deific power. They had painstakingly engraved hunting and worshipping scenes upon the back of the rocks. Centuries later one highwayman had stopped a coach by the commonplace expedient of stretching a lariat across the road at ankle-height. Fortunately the driver had seen the rope at the last moment otherwise there would probably have been a bad upset when the coach-and-six hit that rope.

It was the first holdup in six or seven years which had no aftermath. No one was shot, none of the horses were taken out of harness, none of the passengers were intimidated, and after the solitary robber had briskly and calmly completed his work he had sent the coach on its way without anyone, not even the whip and gun-guard who were atop the coach and therefore had excellent visibility on all sides, seeing any more of the outlaw than his carbine-barrel, his dark hat, and a little of his upper body where it showed around the smooth corner of an ancient stone.

The driver had wheeled off the road a mile on ahead, made a wide sashay so as not to pass those rocks within gun-range, and had boiled back to Morganton with his breathless information.

What the outlaw had gotten off the coach was a leather-and-canvas pouch containing six hundred dollars, surplus cash being sent up to the larger town of Chamberlain, where they had a bank, by several merchants of Morganton including Reg Morgan, Dan Herlihy, Dan Cowper and Abraham Neve, who owned and operated the general store in Morganton.

It was not a fortune in New York or Chicago or even Cincinnati or Cheyenne, but in Morgan Valley six hundred greenbacks in cash was enough money to get by on very comfortably for several years. More to the point, the way in which it had been taken aroused the entire town. Will Chance even had recruits for his posse looking for *him* instead

20

of the other way around.

He led them northward in a swoop, armed to the teeth and bitterly determined, ten tough men including all the individuals who had lost their money, excepting the storekeeper Neve, who had a bad hip even when he walked, and who could not therefore ride for any distance at all astride a horse.

At the rocks they found a solitary carbine bullet standing atop the rounded stone where the highwayman had stood, as though the highwayman did not want anyone to be mistaken about where he had been.

Reg was uncomplimentary. 'Show-off son of a bitch.'

Will kept them away until he had scouted up the boot-tracks all the way around where a horse had been waiting. From there, they rode due west across Ox-Yoke range for two miles on the trail of the highwayman. Then his tracks abruptly halted altogether where they had to ford a low little clear-water creek.

Dan Cowper's sabre-scar was shiny with sweat and brighter red than the other parts of his face by the time they got to that creek. It was hot out and the sunshine was directly upon Will's possemen; there was no shade across the grassland where they were riding.

Dan, who had scouted during the war, made a big gesture. 'He didn't come out of the water; he rode up-creek or down to conceal his tracks. Someone go up-country while I'll go down. Watch very close for the place where he came out. Real close.'

The rest of them forded the watercourse and rode fanned out. They made no attempt to ride swiftly. They had no idea where their prey was and saw no point in wearing out their saddle-animals just to cover a lot of ground.

By the time they saw Dan Cowper's mounted signal far southward and headed in his direction to pick up the tracks again, it was mid-afternoon and Dan was worrying.

'Sure as hell we're not going to overtake him before sunset. Unless we can figure his course before it gets too dark to see his tracks, we're going to lose him in the night.'

They didn't figure his course for an excellent reason: when they were loping overland, eastward, with the fresh tracks directly ahead of them, that outlaw made an abrupt about-face and headed back for the creek where he went down into the water and did not emerge again.

Cowper swore long and hard, then said, 'Northward. The bastard went northward upstream this time. That'd be natural, wouldn't it? Well, bless his lousy soul I'll guess he knows we'll figure it like that, and he'll go southward again.'

'In the dark,' mused Will Chance, levying a long look in the direction of the setting sun.

They split up again and rode the creek-banks, but without much hope because the shadows were coming down on all sides. What they found was that the renegade came out of the creek and this time he rode due west. He was far ahead, they could be certain of that even in the late afternoon light because it was all open country out there; grassland to the horizon, in fact, to the farthest mountains which they could no longer see, and there was no sign of a mounted man to the west. There was no sign of a mounted man in any other direction, for that matter.

They held a council and Cowper, Morgan and Herlihy said they would camp overnight at the creek and head out at first-light in the morning. They were financial losers; they had the best of all powerful motivations to catch up with that highwayman.

The others turned back a little disconsolately. They had boiled out of town in the early morning with such high hopes. No one liked to belly-up to the bar in town and admit failure after a day-long manhunt as part of an official posse. The law, not the lawless, should triumph.

Will was particularly moody on the ride back. He had run down his share of them and this man was a real professional. That worried Will. In the back of his secret mind he doubted that he would be able, this time, to come out of it looking very heroic to his townsmen.

He had a genuine feeling of failure before he had made more than a wide sashay. He'd never had any illusions about this kind of manhunt. Most of the advantage, especially in open territory, was with the fugitive, and providing he was enough of a professional to be well-mounted, and possessed just a rudimentary knowledge of the countryside, he would be just about impossible to run down.

When Will and his riders got back to Morganton the word had spread; even Colonel Hardin and his rangeboss were in town. There were a number of rangemen in town and they were all interested in the progress the law had made. This kind of a robbery was rare and therefore interesting.

Will explained where Dan was, to his nightman, and that news of course was quickly spread among the *Buffalo Saloon*'s patrons.

Will had returned from putting up his horse out back of the jailhouse and was willing to end this day quickly when Devereaux from the corralyard caught him out front and asked about the highwayman. As soon as Will had repeated his story once again Devereaux said, 'Will, that's the first pouch of money I've sent out in a year. Now how did he know it would be on that stage?'

The easiest reply was to say the highwayman probably hadn't known, he had just been lucky. Instead, Will said, 'Henry, have you fired anyone up at the yard lately— maybe within the past week or so?'

Devereaux hadn't. 'I haven't fired a man in

24

six or eight months. You mean you think he was someone who worked for the company?'

'Maybe someone who knew that pouch would be aboard that particular stage,' replied Constable Chance. 'That's what you implied a minute ago when you said you hadn't sent out any money in a year.'

'Well, no,' stated Devereaux, 'I didn't mean maybe the highwayman had ever worked for me here at Morganton. What I was getting at, Will, was that maybe he knew from Dan Cowper or from Neve, or maybe Herlihy about that money being sent out. But not from me; not from working at the way-station because I got a policy: I never tell a soul, especially anyone around the corralyard, that there is to be a pouch of money sent out.'

Will said, 'Well, then he was just a lucky highwayman, Henry. He would have held up that coach anyway.' Will started to move off. It had been a long, arduous, futile day. He was hungry and tired and not a little demoralised.

Devereaux seemed to understand because he said, 'After you've rested up are you going back out?'

Will was indeed going back out. 'In the morning with a fresh horse. By then maybe Herlihy or Cowper or someone anyway, will have found fresh tracks.' Will mechanically smiled and pushed away on his way up the road to the rooming-house. He would have very much enjoyed crossing to the saloon for a nightcap but he saw all the lights, all the saddle animals tied out front and heard all the noise over there. He could never have got his nightcap without being swarmed over by curious stockmen, so he had to forgo the drink and head directly for his room.

Colonel Hardin was sitting on the rooming-house porch smoking a cigar when Constable Chance came up the two low steps heading for the doorway. The colonel removed his cigar to speak.

'Will . . . ?'

Chance turned, peering into the dark.

Hardin pointed to a nearby chair. 'Will; there is something you might be interested in,' the colonel quietly said. 'Sit down for a moment.'

At least this time when he was badgered he could sit down. With Devereaux he'd had to remain standing. As he approached the chair Hardin fished forth a cigar and offered it. Never before had he done anything that friendly in Will Chance's presence, and this time Will declined with a curt head shake. He leaned to look closely at Colonel Hardin, his tiredness now in abeyance while his curiosity came to the fore.

The old man had clearly been sitting here on the porch for some little time. He was alone and he was comfortable, with his coat open, his hat shoved back, and his booted feet hooked atop the low porch railing. In shadows

26

he did not look as old as he had to be.

'Where did the tracks lead you?' he asked, without any preliminary, or without clarifying what he meant.

Will answered succinctly because he understood perfectly. 'They went over your range to the creek, then southward, then back around to that darned creek again. We used all the daylight up following them. Cowper, Morgan and Herlihy stayed out there at the creek to head out first thing ahead of dawn.'

Hardin pulled smoke and trickled it. 'Sounds like he's a professional, Will.'

Chance nodded. 'He is. Did you know how much money he got?'

'Six hundred dollars. It's all over town. Abe Neve was wailing like a lost soul when we rode into town this afternoon.' George Hardin turned. 'What do you think your chances are?'

'Of catching up to him? The same chances a snowball has in hell,' replied Will frankly. 'But I'm not going to give up. Tomorrow when we go out there we'll be fixed for a long trail.'

'And suppose he rode all night?' asked the colonel.

'Then he'll have that much of a lead,' retorted Constable Chance, 'which only means he'll also have one damn tired horse under him, Colonel, and we'll be fresh and riding fresh critters.' Will leaned back a little. 'I've done this before a few times, and there is a system to it. Professional or not, and regardless of whether he escapes me or not, Colonel, there is a routine you follow, and eventually you find him.'

Hardin was interested. 'What kind of a routine?'

'A man with six hundred dollars, a fired horse and a shrunken gut heads for a town, Colonel, or a big ranch—most likely a town—and he eats and sleeps and looks after his horse, then he eats and sleeps some more, and meanwhile I've got queries riding with every damned coach . . . The minute that feller stops, the advantage comes back to me.'

Will arose. 'Every lawman between here and Chamberlain will recognise a shrunken-looking man riding a wore-down horse . . . I'll get him, Colonel. Good night now.'

CHAPTER FOUR

HARDIN's INFORMATION

The following morning Will recalled what the colonel had said. '. . . Something you might be interested in.'

Will had been tired; a man's brain doesn't function well when he's in that shape. Will had not allowed the colonel to explain, instead Will had taken the initiative and had held it, then he had gone off to bed leaving Hardin sitting out there.

It was embarrassing to think back to all this now, but his excuse was valid: he had been dog-tired last night.

Further, he expected to be somewhere within the vicinity of the Ox-Yoke's headquarters today, unless those blasted tracks cut back around to the east again, in which case he would drop in and see Colonel Hardin.

This morning he rode alone. He had not told anyone when he would be leaving, nor had he felt that he would need any more possemen than the three men out at the creek.

It was not a crew of renegades he was after. It was just one man.

It was not quite dark when he left Morganton heading north-westerly in the direction of the creek, but neither was it daylight yet. In fact there would be no daylight for perhaps another couple of hours. He had planned it this way; he wanted to be at the creek-camp just about as the men out there were striking camp.

He had an extra pair of saddlebags along, with food. There was even a pony of fiery brandy in one of the pockets. It was a poor substitute for someone's vanished, stolen money, but it was bound to be welcome among men like Herlihy and Cowper. Morgan, oddly enough for a blacksmith, drank very sparingly.

The morning was chilly. This was of course the most chilly part of the day. Even so it was

29

not an uncomfortable kind of cold; the year was too far advanced by this springtime for genuine cold to be abroad. By the time Will got within sight of the creek-willows but not quite close enough to be able to make out the hobbled horses and the creek-camp, there seemed to be a few degrees of pleasant and welcome warmth coming up-country from the south, riding the low ground-swell force of a fragrant little breeze.

Reg Morgan was at the camp but neither Cowper nor Herlihy were anywhere in sight and neither were their horses.

Morgan, taciturn almost any time but especially so this early in the morning, watched Constable Chance dismount and step ahead to drop the food-laden saddlebags, then he grudgingly said, 'Cowper couldn't stand it last night, just settin' around here and waitin' so he went out and used up all his matches . . . They left me to fetch you along. You ready?'

Will was indeed ready. He retrieved the laden saddle-bags because Reg clearly was not going to do it, then they mounted up and rode south-westerly. Will said, 'They found tracks in the dark?'

Morgan answered curtly. 'You can do anything if you got enough time.' He offered no additional elaboration until Will sighed, rummaged until he found the pony of brandy and handed it over.

'Take a drink,' he growled. 'There's got to

be something that'll improve your lousy disposition, Reg.'

Morgan handed the bottle back untouched, and forced a smile. 'All right; thing is I don't like to talk until after coffee and breakfast. You didn't by any chance . . . ?'

'Coffee? No. But I got tinned sardines and some other stuff.'

The blacksmith rolled a smoke instead, and he continued his valiant effort to improve his early-morning disposition. 'There is something about this highwayman a feller in my line of work would notice. He's ridin' a horse with town-shoes and city-head nails. That means he came from the city; at least the last set of shoes tacked on to his animal was put on in a town by a city smith.'

Will was mildly interested. 'Nearest city would be southward. This feller held up the stage *north* of town.'

Reg was unperturbed. 'No sense in waiting around for a southbound if you knew the northbound would head out first.'

Will said, 'How would he have known?' and remembered his conversation with Henry Devereaux last night. 'How would he know, unless he knew the schedules out of Morganton?'

Reg inhaled, exhaled, looked thoughtfully at the red tip of his cigarette and said, 'He wouldn't, would he?'

They were still walking their horses south-westerly when the first slanting sun-rays came down over the distant rims. It seemed to Will Chance that Cowper and Herlihy had covered an awful lot of ground, for a couple of men who were track-hunting in the dark by moonlight.

Reg said, 'They had all night, and you know those two. Especially Herlihy.'

They came back to the creek and forded it again. Reg sat upon the far side like an Indian, hands clasped atop his saddlehorn, staring stonily at the tracks in the new grass without saying a word. Then he shook his head and they set out again.

Three times they crossed that watercourse and the last time Will swore with feeling because obviously, wherever Cowper and Herlihy were on ahead they too were being led around by the nose, in and out of the creek, up and down it, and eventually when the highwayman got tired of playing this game, he was going to play something else, another game. Will had quiet, strong misgivings long before Reg hoisted an arm.

Miles distant off in the direction of Colonel Hardin's headquarters were a pair of horsemen on the ground standing at the head of their horses, waiting. They had seen Will and Reg long ago, and were now willing to rest until the riders came on up.

Cowper's sabre scar was grey; his entire lower face looked grey and unhealthy, the result of beard-stubble which Will Chance had never seen on his face before. Dan Herlihy's appearance was dishevelled and soiled and exasperated. When Will leaned to hand down the laden saddlebags and Herlihy felt the brandy bottle, he smiled. It was the first pleasant expression from any of them.

Cowper waited for his chance at the food with good patience, and while he stood there he explained about the tracks they had followed all night long.

'I'll kill the son of a bitch if I ever get a chance,' he said, as a sort of statement-of-fact preliminary, then he got down to business.

'Yonder he went, from one side of the creek to the other side, deliberately leaving tracks we could find and follow—hell—even using starlight and matches. The last sign of him heads southward, but I can tell you right now and without leaving this spot that he'll switch course again a couple miles onward . . . You see Ox-Yoke's buildings from here? Well, the way we got this figured he's done one of two things; he's ridden over there and stolen a fresh horse, or he didn't ride over there at all, he turned due east and rode over to town and stole a fresh horse.'

Will swung to earth. If that outlaw had been in Morganton stealing a horse this morning early, Will was also there and maybe they had even heard one another. If the townsfolk learned of something like this they would never allow Will to forget it.

He said, 'I'll help you kill the son of a bitch, if we ever get the chance. Well; you fellers can eat in the saddle. Suppose we ride over to Ox-Yoke so's you two can borrow a couple of fresh animals too.'

Reg Morgan, who had been taciturnly silent throughout all this, finally made a remark as the four of them reined over in Ox-Yoke's direction.

'If we ever catch him you'd better pray he's not as good with guns as he is at laying tracks, because if he is . . .'

Morgan did not finish it.

They headed for Ox-Yoke, which was not a long ride, and when they reached the yard there were two men in sight, one was the cook, over on the porch of his rambling log cookhouse and dining-hall, the other was Colonel Hardin leaning thoughtfully upon the tie-rack out front of a big log barn. He looked small and almost frail with that barn for a background.

He had his hat shoved back and was wearing a grey coat, grey trousers, and no bulletbelt nor sixgun. When he finally recognised them Hardin shoved up a trifle straighter on the hitchrail and fished for a cigar.

The cook, who had been draping grey dishtowels over a length of stretched lariat upon his porch, did not nod as the possemen went by, which was not unusual for him; he was a sour-tempered man named Padgett with poor circulation in his feet which made him flop when he walked rather than step out. They all knew him.

Otherwise the big yard was empty, as it was supposed to be at this time of day. Ox-Yoke's riding crew should by now be well at work out upon the range somewhere.

Hardin welcomed them with a tentative smile and a sucked back set of lips, as though he were performing some social grace because it was required of him, not because his heart was in it.

When he gestured for them to dismount he looked from man to man, and ended up by addressing Will Chance.

'In my time I've had occasion to manhunt a few, and if you don't get a sound lead on them within eight hours, you just about aren't ever going to even see their dust.'

Will dismounted wearing a wooden smile. He let that rough statement pass and asked if they could borrow a couple of fresh horses.

Colonel Hardin motioned towards a big circular corral. 'Help yourself; those are sound, using horses over there, well-broke and tough.' He watched Will send his riders in that direction, and when Will faced him again Colonel Hardin had a pithy comment to offer.

'Will, that man you're looking for has at least one friend in town.'

The constable accepted this and decided it

had been what Hardin had tried to tell him last night. 'I figure you're probably right,' he replied. 'At first I figured it was someone Devereaux might have fired a few days ago. Someone who would know about the northbound coach carrying that money-pouch. But he hasn't fired anyone and no one's quit.'

Colonel Hardin trickled cigar smoke without taking his eyes off Will Chance. 'Yesterday a couple of my riders saw a stranger on our north-westerly range. When they loped over, he left them like they were tied to a tree. He was a very well-mounted man. They looked up his sign. He was riding a town-shod horse. That made him a plumb stranger. Later, when we heard about the robbery we figured out who that stranger had been.'

'Did you go looking for him?'

Colonel Hardin shook his head. 'This is a cattle ranch not a school for embryonic possemen. No, we didn't go looking and if we had he wouldn't have been anywhere around. But when Waite and I were heading for town last night we cut the sign of a man riding city horseshoes. He was also heading for town, but first he zigzagged back and forth across the creek west of here—the one we call Grass Creek.'

Will frowned. 'How far did you follow his tracks?'

'If you hadn't been so all-fired set on getting

to bed last night I'd have told you. We followed that man's sign right down into Morganton.'

'You're sure it was the same set of tracks?'

Hardin removed his cigar, expectorated, plugged the stogie back between strong, ground-down square teeth and glared.

Will nodded. 'All right. The rest of it is that you figure someone in town may be hiding this feller.'

'Yup. If that outlaw went to town, my guess is that he already had it fixed so's he could hide out for a week or so. Until the ruckus dies down anyway. That would be sound strategy—if he didn't want to try and outrun a posse, and I'd say he didn't want to do that or he wouldn't have been so busy laying false trails yesterday.'

Will turned to watch his men leading forth two freshly-saddled horses from the corral-area. 'I'm obliged,' he said to the colonel without looking at him. 'Not much point in riding all over hell, then. We'll head back for town and see if we can get some kind of lead on that feller—and his friends.'

Hardin said no more. He continued to lean upon the hitchrail though and watch as the possemen mounted up. He nodded to them when they called back that they would take care of his horses and return them directly. He nodded and smoked and narrowly watched them ride out of his yard without saying a word.

37

CHAPTER FIVE

THE PROBLEM

The other men listened to everything Will had to say as they went back by the creek to pick up that sign again.

Dan Herlihy was of the opinion that those tracks Waite Culpepper and George Hardin had seen leading right on down into town had to belong to the highwayman.

Reg Morgan agreed with that. It was Dan Cowper who said, 'Just why in hell would someone go to all that bother laying tracks back and forth and up and down like that feller did, when all he ever had to do was cut far out and around then ride right on up into town?'

Reg answered tartly. 'Because he wanted to wait until nightfall—why else? No highwayman's stupid enough to ride into a town near where he's just raided a coach, on the darned same day—in broad daylight.'

They did not find the tracks again for almost an hour, then Will came across them, and to one side of them another couple of sets. Those, he said, had undoubtedly been made by Hardin and Waite Culpepper.

It fitted very nicely so they rode along in the rising new-day warmth watching tracks and discussing what the highwayman was up to, and also speculating about who might be protecting him in town.

Reg said, ' Probably the darned Secesh,' and got a quick glare from Will who rarely allowed one of those unpleasant allusions to go by unchallenged. Reg saw the look and shrugged. 'Or maybe some Yankee.'

That time he got a glare from Dan Herlihy the former Union infantryman. Cowper might have also glared except that he was busy rolling a smoke. Dan Cowper had also been a Union soldier. He had that crescent-shaped scar to prove it.

They finally crossed trampled ground not far from Morganton's outskirts and from here it became very difficult to keep track of the sign. There were too many tracks. Maybe an Indian could have done it but they did not have one along, and even that wasn't much of a certainty any more. A lot of Indians were cowboys and freighters and horsemen nowadays; very few ever bothered to learn the old skills from their fathers.

Eventually, within hearing distance of town, they lost the tracks altogether and rode the last three-quarters of a mile without bothering to try and find them in the trampled dust and hoof-scarred dun soil.

They agreed among themselves to say absolutely nothing to a living soul about their suspicion that the highwayman was being cleverly hidden in town. In fact they agreed among themselves not to discuss their man-hunt at all, except to deliberately give the impression that they had lost the tracks and were almost ready to give up the hunt. If any story at all filtered down to the highwayman and the man who was hiding him, it should be one which pointed up the demoralisation of the possemen.

Will's last order was for the three of them to meet him at his jailhouse office that evening after supper. Not that he expected to have anything startling to tell them, but he wanted to keep those three men—good hands every one of them—up to date on what was happening, and he also wanted to have them loose if he needed them.

They separated on Main Street heading in different directions to care for their saddle-stock. Will went to the shed out back of the jailhouse and off-rigged, forked feed into the manger, and as he was replacing the hayfork a thought arrived which bothered him a little.

Colonel Hardin and Waite Culpepper had followed those city-shoes right down into town last night. Up until this morning there had not been much actual fresh traffic out along the west side of town. There had been a lot of *old* tracks and indications of *old* movement, saddle-stock, wagons and buggies, and even some human boot-track marks, but no fresh sign . . . Then how had Colonel Hardin and his

40

rangeboss tracked someone right down into town by *fresh tracks*?

Will, Morgan, Herlihy and Cowper were not good trackers but they knew fresh sign when they saw it—and they had not found any which was closer than half a mile to town, from the west, from the direction Colonel Hardin had tracked the highwayman.

Hell; there hadn't been any fresh tracks out there!

Will finished hanging up the hayfork and instead of going to the cafe or even on around to his jailhouse-office he struck out back up through the west-side alley and spent more than an hour on foot slow-pacing his way back and forth from north to south, and he even walked out about a half mile without finding any fresh shod horse-sign.

He found three sets of barefoot pony tracks, and he even saw the three youngsters riding their shaggy little mustangs who had made them, but he found no other sign at all, and that troubled him.

He went round to the saloon expecting to find Dan Herlihy behind his bar, but the substitute barman shook his head. 'Dan's sleeping. You must have rode 'em a hard trail, Constable.'

Will got a foamy glass of beer and took it down the bar where the pickles and sliced cold beef were. He was making a sandwich down there when Reg Morgan walked in, saw him, and ambled over to say, 'Something come to me down at the shop, Will . . . Didn't you tell us Colonel Hardin and Waite Culpepper followed those city-head nails right down here into town?'

Will nodded and moved to one side a little in case Reg also wanted to make a sandwich. Reg didn't, but he pulled out his makings to roll a smoke while awaiting Will's reply.

'I told you exactly that,' stated the lawman, 'and that's exactly what George Hardin told me.'

'Damn it,' grumbled Morgan, 'There were no fresh tracks. Didn't we have to give up on them a half mile or more out?'

Will smiled and bit down into his sandwich, then tried to speak around his mouthful. 'Yeah. I just finished making a second inspection out there.'

'You figure Hardin was lying—too?'

Will chewed and swallowed before answering. 'I figure he may have *thought* he was following the fresh sign of a highwayman, Reg. Or maybe—'

'Gawddammit,' said the blacksmith, ' don't play mamby-pamby with me. That old bastard was lying. He's always saying how much he knows, how many men he's tracked, how all that soldiering he did as a Secesh officer taught him how to read sign and all. Will; *there were no tracks.* You and Cowper and Herlihy and me all saw that . . . Why would a man like

42

that lie? He's rich, owns more land than you can shake a stick at, runs cattle between here and the lousy horizon, hires good men and pays up. Then why would he lie about one lousy highwayman and our lousy six hundred dollars?'

Will chewed, washed down the food with beer, chewed some more and signalled for the barman to fetch up another tankard of beer for Reg Morgan. He did all this without answering, and Morgan accepted the beer with a dour nod, willing to allow his friend time enough to finish his sandwich or fabricate his reply, whichever came first.

Eventually Will said, 'I don't know why he told us that story. I *do* know that he tried to waylay me last night on the rooming-house porch to make darned sure I heard that yarn— and I didn't give him the chance, so he told it to me this morning at the ranch.'

Reg sipped beer and dolorously gazed at the back-bar.

Will continued to speak. 'Something else I know. Colonel Hardin don't say anything unless he has a reason for saying it.'

Morgan bobbed his head. 'For a fact,' he averred.

'Reg; all of a sudden it don't seem as important to me where that highwayman is being hidden, as it does that George Hardin is somehow or other mixed up in it. And there's one more thing: Where we lost that man's sign is exactly where I'd try to lose my tracks if I had in mind leading possemen on a wild-goose chase over to a town—*before I turned back.*'

Reg slowly turned and slowly drained his beer glass. 'Turned back,' he muttered, placing the emptied glass atop the bar. 'I'll be damned. Turned back as soon as he got up where we couldn't track him—because he didn't leave no tracks up there—and he rode west again . . . Will?'

'To Ox-Yoke,' said the lawman softly. 'Reg; he played back-and-forth on us for ten miles, and he constantly headed southward while he was doing it. He rode east then west, then east and west again, and all the damned time he was also going south, wasn't he? Well, where we finally left him to go borrow a couple of horses we had Ox-Yoke in sight. So did he. A man with a posse on his trail heads for his shelter. He sashays to throw off the posse but mainly he heads for his shelter, don't he?'

Reg said, 'Ox-Yoke, for Chris'sake?' He had already arrived at a conclusion that George Hardin had not told the truth, which clearly meant that Hardin was somehow involved with the outlaw—but going far enough to suggest that Hardin might actually be shielding the outlaw was something else.

Will looked down the bar, and back. 'Are you pretty busy at the forge?' he asked. 'Someone should go out there and spy on the place.'

Morgan did not reply for a moment, he stepped closer and began putting together a sandwich, scowling all the while. '. . . All right, I'll do it,' he murmured, still concentrating on the sandwich. 'But that's open country out there. I'll have to take my spyglass and maybe sit in the willows back at the creek and do it like that.'

'If they catch you, Reg, you'll have a hell of a time convincing them you went out there to fish the creek. Folks don't fish much using spyglasses.'

Morgan looked at Will with mild disgust. 'I didn't come down in the last rain,' he growled.

Later, when Will Chance went back to his office Abe Neve from the general store came over. Abe had been watching the jailhouse from his storefront window, waiting for Will to arrive across the road. He knew the possemen had returned, and he had heard all the stories the possemen had told. His general store was more than just the point of distribution for the post, and a source of supply for just about everything people in Morgan Valley needed, it was also the clearing-house for rumours, gossip, and titillating secrets. But Abe was an individual who liked to get his stories directly from a reliable source when he could.

What he wanted to know now was whether or not it was true what folks were discreetly saying about a lawman who should not be in town at all, but who should be out riding over

45

the countryside hell for leather in pursuit of the highwayman who had made off with some of Abe Neve's money.

Will smiled at the smaller and older man. 'What are they saying, Abe?'

Neve looked away and back again. 'It don't matter. What I want to know, Will, is whether you have any hopes of finding that man and getting our money back.'

Will had hopes. 'Sure, Abe, I figure I'll manage it.'

'Here? Sitting around here in town?'

Will kept smiling. 'Maybe. This would be the closest place for the outlaw to spend his money, wouldn't it?'

'That's ridiculous,' exclaimed the storekeeper. 'He wouldn't dare. Folks are looking for a stranger as it is, and if one come along with bulging pockets . . . Will, I've always had faith in you. I've stood up for you over my counter many a time.'

'I appreciate that,' said the taller man.

'But right now I'm getting a little doubtful, Will. Right now I'm thinking maybe that Henry could be right when he says you aren't going about this right.'

Will sighed, arose and reached for his hat off the antler rack. 'Abe, you and Henry are good at the store and the way-station. Did I ever try and tell you how to run your business?'

The storekeeper did not reply, he instead

walked to the door then turned back to say, 'All right. I'll trust in you, Will, and I'll tell Henry he'd ought to do that too. But if you don't get my money back I'm going to be downright disappointed.'

Will waited until Neve had departed, had closed the door after himself, then he dumped the hat upon the back of his head and also left the office, but Will went northward while Abe went almost directly across the road to his store.

Will went up to Charley Graham's telegraph-franchise office to send away a telegram to the War Department in Washington, D.C.

CHAPTER SIX

A LONG NIGHT

Out in the back room behind Dan Cowper's apothecary and undertaking shop there were two five-gallon open crocks. Perhaps it was not common for a druggist to make beer in his back room but there were not very many individuals who came so well-endowed to the task; apothecaries were natural, or at least they were trained chemists.

Perhaps professional brewmasters might question that this qualification was an attribute in a highly specialised field, but Dan Cowper thought it was, and so did quite a number of dedicated beer-drinkers around Morganton.

That is where Cowper was that evening after supper when Constable Chance went in search of him. Cowper had just started a fresh batch and was solicitously making absolutely sure that it got all the heat—but never too much heat—that was required to ensure the fermentation would ensue neither too slowly nor too rapidly. As he explained to Will Chance, the difference was a matter of proper curing as opposed to improper curing; if there was not enough heat it might take as long as twenty-five days before the bottling could take place and if there was too much heat the fermentation might be complete in just a few days in which case the beer had a 'green' taste.

Will was not the least bit interested but he had learned some years back that the best way to get along with people who were more or less fanatical about something was to allow them to get it all said. Will listened, sniffed, and tried to decide whether what he was smelling was formaldehyde or fermenting malt and hops.

When he got the opportunity, eventually, to explain why he had come down to Cowper's shop, Dan took him out front, closed the back-room door, and got them both a glass of beer.

He listened to everything Will had to say, then shook his head. 'Why would someone like George Hardin protect a highwayman?' he asked, and Will had to give the same reply he had been giving to himself.

'I don't have much of an idea, Dan. Moneywise it don't make a lick of sense. Otherwise, a man could stand here and figure out a dozen reasons which *might* be the answer, but maybe not even get close. And I can't prove right at this minute that Colonel Hardin really is hiding anyone. All I can prove is what you and Reg and Herlihy and I know for a fact. After the colonel told us those tracks came right down into town, and he and Waite followed them on in, we discovered otherwise.'

'Why would he tell that particular lie?' Dan Cowper wanted to know. 'He had to figure we'd head back for town and do some tracking on our own.'

'Maybe he figured we'd take his word for it. Maybe he figured we'd do what we did—track those marks right up to within three-quarters of a mile or so from the west side of town, then lose them in the trampled ground out yonder—which is pretty much what we did.'

Cowper came up with an idea which was too late by one full day. 'What we should have done was scout around out near Ox-Yoke's headquarters and pick up the sign out there— if it went into the yard, out there.'

Will shrugged. If Hardin were indeed hiding the highwayman, he would have smoothed out all signs of the man's having arrived in the ranchyard. Nevertheless that opened up a fresh avenue for speculation. Maybe someone out there—Waite Culpepper, or the ranch-cook, or one of Ox-Yoke's rangemen, had seen the stranger ride in. At least one of them might have seen that outlaw's horse.

'All I know for a fact,' he told the druggist, 'Is that Colonel Hardin told us he did something that we now know he did not do, Dan. The other plumb fact seems to me to be that this highwayman didn't leave the country. It don't even look to me like he tried to leave the country.'

Cowper nodded. 'Which makes it seem like he maybe never intended to leave after stopping Henry's coach. But I'll tell you something, Will, if that feller hadn't stopped the stage we never would have known he even knew the colonel.'

'If he came here to visit the colonel,' added Will, 'why in hell did he rob a stage and put the colonel on the hot seat?' Will did not really invite an answer to that, he instead reverted to their earlier discussion and emphasised that he might need the co-operation of Cowper and Morgan and Herlihy, but especially of Cowper and Herlihy, in the event some of the things the law now had to do in its continuing investigation required support.

Dan Cowper looked a trifle sceptical. 'What kind of support? If you mean with guns—hell, Will—old Hardin has never hired riders who weren't gunhandy, and what do fellers like a blacksmith or a saloonman or an apothecary have, to face up against fellers like that with?'

'Maybe it'll never come to that,' speculated Will. 'Anyway, what I need is prompt backing if I need Cowper understood, but although he assented, promising in fact to help supply that support, he continued to look doubtful, even when he brought forth two more bottles of his dark lager, and the conversation got around to what obligations citizens might have in the areas of supplying active support to the officials they elected to office.

The lager helped at resolving this mild argument. Dan Cowper had always admired Will Chance's ability to neutralise the undercurrent of Secesh-Yank antagonism in Morgan Valley, and this, plus the beer, eventually induced him to abandon his doubtful stand and come out in favour of total support for the law.

Will had never for a moment doubted but that the apothecary with the sabre-scarred left cheek would help him. Nor was he convinced he would need help, but when a man went up against the richest, biggest and most powerful cowman in an area, he had better make certain in advance that he was not going to have to do all that by himself, badge or no badge.

After leaving Cowper's shop Will returned to the locality of Herlihy's saloon, but he did not enter because he knew what Herlihy would say in response to Will's appeal for active support. Also because the place was packed with rangemen, this being Saturday night, and Herlihy would be as busy as a kitten in a box of shavings, unable to discuss affairs alien to his profession.

Saturday night probably wasn't even the time to go talk to Dan Cowper, but Will had done it, and now he paused upon the opposite side of the road to roll a smoke and to savour the very pleasant, warmly relaxing glow two bottles of Cowper's homebrew had induced inside him.

He lit up, exhaled, and slouched there watching the trickle of rangeriders in and out of the saloon across from him. One cowboy was rubbery-legged and two of his friends were herding him out to their horses at the tie-rack.

There was a town ordinance against drunks. Will smoked and watched, and felt no compulsion to do a thing until one of those more sober rangeriders said, 'Lon, you dang fool, you heard what Waite said about no one getting smoked up, because we got that big gather come Monday. And look at you.'

Will dropped the smoke, stepped on it as he propelled himself forward into the roadway from the east-side plankwalk, and made his thrusting way in among the drowsing, tethered animals over yonder.

One of those cowboys saw him coming and muttered a warning under his breath. The other cowboy, in the act of boosting Lon astride a saddle, looked around, then loosened his grip as Will came on up, stopped to look long at Lon, then say, 'Why in hell didn't you get him out of town?'

One of the Ox-Yoke riders smiled weakly, 'That's what we was fixin' to do right now, Marshal. He ain't bothersome, just drunk is all.'

Will jerked his head. 'Down that way,' he said, his meaning abundantly clear.

'Oh hell,' piped up the second Ox-Yoke cowboy, 'He ain't done anything and we was about to haul him away so's no one would be upset. Marshal, you don't have to lock him up.'

Will moved out of the way and jerked his head. 'There's a damned town ordinance,' he explained. 'Hike him on down there.'

'Who would know?' asked one of the complaining riders.

Will said, 'I would. Now let's get on down there.'

One of those Ox-Yoke men muttered an earthy exclamation of deep-down disgust, helped his companion hoist Lon between them and start down the wide roadway. As they were walking along Will studied the inebriated man. He was youthful, wiry, tanned from long exposure in all kinds of weather, and durable-looking. Will asked his full name and got a growled retort.

'Lon Stearn.'

'I don't think I've seen him around town before,' said Will, and the other cowboy looked up with sullen hostility showing.

'All that means, Marshal, is that you set around town too much. He hired on two months ago, before Jack and me did. He was riding for the colonel before we got to know the range. He's harmless and he's a decent feller to-boot, and now you'll likely get him fired for being locked up.'

'Hardin can have him back in the morning when he sobers up,' said Will, moving around to reach the jailhouse door and open it for the supporters of Lon Stearn.

Nothing more was said. The indignant rangeriders stood owlishly while Will emptied the drunk cowboy's pockets, put it all into the cowboy's hat, then took his prisoner down to a small cell to drop him upon the straw mattress and lock him in.

One of the riders wanted to know what the fine would be and Will told him there wouldn't be any. 'All he's got to do is sober up. I'll see to his horse directly, and in the morning when he's able he can head for home . . . That's the way it's got to be. Sorry gents.'

After those cowboys departed Will went up, got the saddle animal and took it around back to his own horse-shed and corrals, off-saddled it, forked feed in to the separate corral from his own animal, and went back inside the jailhouse.

The last time he had invoked that ordinance against drunks being in town had been two years back when a cowboy tried to shoot out the road-lights. Since then he had looked the other way when at least two dozen drunks who were harmless had gone unsteadily about their business. But none of them had possessed the same potential the cowboy named Lon Stearn possessed.

It was only a shot in the dark but under the circumstances Will wanted to exploit each opportunity. He poured black java down that cowboy until Lon had to be escorted out back into the alleyway, and after that he poured more coffee down him, almost relentlessly. Eventually the coffee—or maybe it was simply a self-defence mechanism—seemed to help the sobering-up process.

Lon sat slumped in a chair in the front office breathing as though he had run an uphill mile and looking unhappily at his boot-toes. Will refilled his coffee cup.

'I got that damned stuff coming out my ears,' the cowboy protested. 'I ain't going to drink any more.'

Will was agreeable. He put aside the pot, offered Lon the makings, and when the cowboy declined Will rolled the cigarette and handed it over. That time Lon accepted.

He seemed to feel better once Will stopped pouring black coffee down him. The cigarette helped as undoubtedly did the pleasant warmth of the constable's office. Lon looked bad, but that went along with what he had almost succeeded in doing to himself.

As he smoked he gradually straightened back in the chair to study Will Chance. 'Why didn't you just leave me sleep it off?' he asked, and got an ambiguous answer.

'Didn't want you to be sick all day tomorrow so's you couldn't make it to the gather on Monday. I can tell you for a fact old George Hardin don't tolerate it when a rider can't come up to scratch after a Saturday night in town.'

Lon looked disgusted. 'Marshal; confound it all, I can carry my whisky.'

'You weren't doing too good a job of it last night.'

'I been that bad off before here in town and you never jumped me, and I've seen fellers in a heap worse shape and you never jumped them neither.'

Will smiled. 'The smart ones stayed out of sight. I don't go out of my way to stall drunks, Lon, but when they get to boldly pushing it into my face, why then I don't have any choice . . . Care for a game of checkers?'

Lon screwed up his face. 'I can't figure you out,' he said plaintively. 'No, I don't want to play no damned game of checkers, just let me get back down there to my cell and get some rest.'

Will kept right on smiling while he dug out the checker-board and gestured for his prisoner to haul his chair closer to the desk.

CHAPTER SEVEN

CONFIRMATION—ON SUNDAY!

Lon Stearn was not a checker-player. He told that to Will and was quietly ignored so in the end he swore and yanked the chair to the desk-top and watched Will set up the black-and-red board, line up the black-and-red checkers, then give his hands a rub together as he raised his eyes.

'Your move,' he said to the cowboy. 'I always let the prisoners have first jump.'

Stearn sulkily considered the board and shoved forward a random checker. 'If I'd known all this was going to happen I never would have even rode into town tonight,' he grumbled. 'Is there an ordinance says I got to play checkers with you?'

'It's a good game,' exclaimed the constable. 'They used to play lots of it out at Ox-Yoke. Maybe now that the colonel's got a house-guest he don't sit in much any more.'

Lon Stearn watched Will move, watched the

opportunity develop and hitched a little closer as he leaned to establish an ambush.

Will kept right on talking as he moved his checker. 'I never sat in on any of the games at the main-house out there but I've heard they used to have some big games. Waite and the colonel and one or two other fellers.'

Lon could have been deaf. He was leaning forward and when Will moved Lon pounced. He jumped two men, one slightly to one side and to the rear of the first man.

Then Lon looked up disbelievingly. He was a man who never gambled and won, not even at checkers. Will appeared momentarily crestfallen but he made a swift and good-natured recovery.

'You've been practising,' he told Stearn. 'Like hell you don't play checkers. You're probably one of them at the main-house.'

Stearn slowly wagged his head. 'I never been inside the main-house, let alone been asked over to play checkers. I don't think the colonel plays anyway, and I know for a fact they don't play checkers at the bunk-house. Poker and blackjack, but not—'

Will jumped one of Lon's checkers. As he picked up the piece Will sighed. 'I expect his house-guest interrupted things at the ranch,' he murmured, and settled both elbows upon the table while watching his opponent.

Lon scowled and pinched his lips together in hard thought. There was an opportunity;

Will Chance had set it up. Lon missed seeing it and made a cautious move. Will set up another opportunity and that time Lon snapped at it, snatched another of Will's checkers, and finally smiled broadly full of unsettling alcohol and coffee, or not.

Then he looked up. 'What house-guest? What are you talking about, a house-guest?'

'The stranger at the ranch,' Will stated. 'The feller who showed up about yesterday.'

Lon stepped unerringly into this larger more important trap too, when he said, 'Oh, that man. Well, I wouldn't know nothin' about him. I don't even know if he's still at the ranch. I only saw the big black horse in the separate corral and the strange outfit on the saddle-pole in the barn . . . Well; you going to move or just set there?'

Will reverted to the earlier trap in order to draw Lon's attention to it. Then he moved to create a double-play and waited, but this time Lon saw it without any help. He chuckled and waggled his head reprovingly. 'You're a sly cuss,' he averred, and moved a checker which could not be captured.

They played for fifteen minutes, Lon won and grumbled bitterly when Will folded the board and put it away. He accused Will of being a poor loser and Will smiled. 'Care for some coffee?'

Lon arose looking uncertain. The last thing he wanted in this world was more coffee, but he was not certain Will might not force him to drink it. Instead, Will accompanied him down to his cell, locked him in and went back up front to roll a smoke and savour it as the town outside got steadily more quiet as the night advanced.

Sure as shooting Colonel Hardin *was* hiding the stage-robber!

When he had finished the cigarette he got his hat and, locking the office after himself, ambled up to make his final round of the night. There were still a dozen or so rangemen at Herlihy's place, and another five or six were standing around out front near the hitchrack, talking and smoking, acting as though it were not midnight and as though they did not have jobs and bunk-houses to ride back to.

Will went home, finally, bedded down, and although he slept like a child, when he opened his eyes in the morning his mind had somehow or other come to a conclusion without his conscious effort.

Reg should know by now whether that house-guest of Hardin's had left the ranch. If he hadn't, then Will had the authority to ride in with a gun, if he had to, kick down a door or two and make an arrest.

He also had the authority to ride out there with several armed men and quietly haul in Colonel Hardin for sheltering a fugitive, for interfering with a peace officer in the performance of his duty by lying to Will the

60

previous day, and maybe also for resisting, which Hardin was certain to do.

The conclusion Will awakened with was simply to release Lon Stearn this morning and ride back to Ox-Yoke with him. Lon would provide him with an excuse to visit the ranch and from there on Will would have to improvise, but he was confident enough to believe, once he was out there, he would be able to find something—maybe that horse Lon had mentioned—to use as a wedge into Colonel Hardin's involvement.

He had no illusions about what might follow after he had involved George Hardin, but that was borrowing trouble; that was worrying about something which was beyond what he initially might do. A wise man took just one step at a time and made sure that first step was the right one before he made preparations to take the next step.

Will ate an early breakfast in a town which was still sleeping, or if it weren't sleeping was just shaking itself awake when he went down to the cafe beyond Herlihy's saloon and rattled the door.

The cafeman was a hulking older man, a rangeman of many years standing whose cafe walls were covered with pictures of men and outfits he had ridden with, and a few bad but representative pictures of the territories he had ridden over.

Like all lifelong stockmen, the cafeman was

an early riser. He opened the door for Constable Chance, waved him to the counter and said, 'Your conscience wouldn't let you sleep. I know how it is.' Then he laughed and headed for his curtained-off kitchen, and for a moment there was no sound but the noise of grease sputtering in a big iron skillet, then the door opened and closed and Will craned around.

Reg Morgan stamped in looking rumpled and unshaven and bleak. Unlike the big cafeman, the blacksmith was unfit for human companionship until after he had eaten, and from the looks of his expression he not only hadn't had breakfast he probably hadn't had supper the night before either.

He glowered at Will, stepped over the bench, sank down and growled loudly. 'Hey, Les! you got any of your lousy hot coffee?'

The cafeman peered from behind his curtained-off kitchen opening, recognised Morgan and smiled broadly. Clearly, the cafeman was not an individual who could be easily annoyed.

He brought two cups of black coffee, winked at Will and jerked his head in Reg's direction, then rolled up his eyes in pantomime and shuffled back to the kitchen.

Will did not make a sound until Reg had finished the coffee, then he asked if Reg had seen anything out yonder where he had been keeping an eye on Ox-Yoke with his brass spyglass.

Reg cursed with considerable feeling before explaining. 'Did you know that the sun reflects off the glass in the front of those spyglasses?'

Will hadn't known this but he could believe it was entirely feasible.

Reg did not allow enough time to pass for Will to comment before he also said, 'They snuck in from behind and the first I even knew they was around at all was when someone cocked a gun maybe fifty feet behind me, and I turned around.'

The cafeman appeared with two thick white platters heaped with fried eggs, a breakfast steak, and mounds of tan-gold fried potatoes. He went back with their cups to refill them and this gave Will his chance.

'Ox-Yoke?' he asked succinctly, and Reg nodded as he picked up his fork.

'They'd seen the reflection off my spyglass and had skirted 'way out and around. Will; that was damned embarrassing.'

'Was it the rangeboss or the colonel?'

'One of 'em was the rangeboss, yes, but the other two was just cowboys.' Reg swallowed, awaited the delayed reaction of his taste buds, then dived into the mounded food for more. 'I thought for a minute I was going to have to take on all three of them. Waite was mad and the cowboys was indignant about someone spyin' on the ranch.'

'What did you tell them?' asked Will.

Reg was clearly chagrined over what he had to say now. 'I lied like a trooper. Said I hadn't been spyin' on the ranch, I was out there trying to catch sight of some lost saddle-horses from town which folks had last seen heading towards the creek from west of town.' Reg swallowed. 'They didn't believe me.'

Will could understand that. It wasn't much of a story, but then he couldn't think of anything which would have been better right at the moment, either, so he went to work also eating breakfast and outside someone rang the bell of the steeple at the north-west end of town where the community church stood.

The sun was bright, the sky was flawless, there was warmth coming into the new day, and finally a few people appeared dressed in their Sunday-best ready for church.

The cafeman came out and jokingly asked if his two customers were going up yonder to sing psalms. He got a steady unamused look from Reg Morgan so he went back into his kitchen.

Reg said, 'In case you forgot why you made me go out there and hide in the lousy creek-willows like a skulking In'ian, there is a stranger at the main-house.'

Will leaned back. 'You saw him?'

'Yeah, right early yesterday morning, and again about ten o'clock after the riding crew had went out onto the range. The second time he came out the colonel was with him and they

64

went around behind the sheds and buildings to reach the barn. They acted like they didn't want the cook to see them from across the yard.'

Will's interest was heightened. 'Could you see him very well?'

'It was a fair distance,' replied the blacksmith, 'but then that's a good spyglass . . . He's maybe thirty, a little taller than the colonel, and wore dark britches and a dark hat. Looked like just another rangerider, except for the way he and the colonel acted, and except for the way he's living in the main-house instead of the bunkhouse.'

Reg continued to eat and drink coffee. His mood improved as time passed and by the time he and Will were just about finished with breakfast, and the person up yonder had stopped ringing that church-bell, Reg was beginning to become a little expansive.

'When Waite and those riders caught me last night I was tempted to ask them who that feller was.'

Will scowled. 'You asked them?'

'No, but I sure was tempted.' Reg rolled a smoke. 'I don't think they got any idea the old man's hiding someone at the main-house. If he was real careful about letting the feller leave the house while his riders were around, and made a big effort to make sure even the cook didn't see him, sure as hell he didn't let Waite and the others know, wouldn't you say ?'

65

Will did not reply to the question. 'I'm going out there this morning.' He explained about Lon Stearn in his jailhouse, and what he proposed using Lon for. Reg listened, sipped coffee, and when Will dumped silver atop the counter to pay for his breakfast and arose, Reg did the same, gulping down the last of his coffee.

Outside, the new-day light was pristine, the town was very quiet and strollers, mostly with children along were parading in the direction of the church. One woman turned from across the road, glared archly at the pair of armed men out front of the cafe in their everyday attire, made a sniffing motion and marched steadily ahead beside her husband with her head slightly elevated in proper Sunday scorn.

Will sighed. Reg was not the least perturbed. Up yonder someone gave the bell-rope a couple of hard tugs, musical sound pealed out over town as the last call to Sunday services reverberated endlessly across all the empty cow range of Morgan Valley, then the silence returned again.

CHAPTER EIGHT

OX-YOKE

Lon Stearn ate like a horse and said nothing, not even to the good-natured big cafeman who sympathetically commiserated, by recalling a few times in his career when he too had been jugged by zealous town constables.

When they were back outside in the empty roadway, Lon rolled a smoke, looked doubtfully at Will and said, 'Thanks for the breakfast—if it come out of your poke.'

They went around behind the jailhouse to saddle up. Lon was impressed by the complete silence. He had not been in Morganton early on a Sunday morning before. When they were riding up the back-alley along the west side of town and the choir-singing came mutedly and sweetly down to them, Lon was even more impressed.

They loped a mile before settling to a steady walk. Lon said, 'That's what a man ought to do. Go to church and live in town and dress decent.'

'And raise a brood,' stated Will, watching the sun's golden brilliance spread and spread.

Lon looked up. 'You don't have to get married just to live decent and go to church.'

Will turned his head. 'No, I expect you

don't. But single men in towns get just like old boar pigs after some years. You might as well stay out on the range.'

Stearn looked disgusted. 'You even got to argue on Sundays,' he grumbled, and spat aside, before fishing for his tobacco sack and cigarette papers. 'I wouldn't have your lousy job for all the gold in Messico. And that is a plumb fact!'

They made fair time. When they reached the creek and had to weave in among the willows to find a decent ford, the sun was very close to its meridian. There were thousands of flies in the shade along the creek hiding from direct sunlight and waiting in there until cattle came to drink. They irreverently pounced upon the pair of mounted men, and their horses.

On the far side of the creek, though, those blood-sucking flies abandoned the riders and flew back into the cool shade of the willows.

Lon looked far ahead towards the Ox-Yoke buildings and let go with a great sigh. 'The colonel might fire me. At least he'll raise hell with me. If today was *tomorrow,* hell, I wouldn't even ride back except to pick up my bedroll and gatherings . . . For what? Two or three lousy little sips of whisky, and a real zealot for a town constable.'

Will nodded. 'You got it figured just about right. I usually don't haul 'em back to the ranch. I usually take 'em onto that mountain north-east of town and nail 'em to a cross up there.'

Lon was not amused. 'Very funny,' he said, then raised an arm. 'Someone is bringin' in a remuda.'

It was true, but the dust and the distance hid the fact that perhaps more than one rider was chousing in those fractious horses. Will was interested. 'How come on Sunday; if you got to use 'em tomorrow why didn't someone fetch them in yesterday?'

Lon shrugged. 'Ask Waite or the colonel. I only ride for the outfit—maybe.'

But when they reached the yard Will did not mention the horses. He rode to the rack out front of the main-house, swung down just as Colonel Hardin emerged onto the veranda, and they exchanged a curt little nod.

Lon had peeled off back a ways and was now riding around behind the horse barn in the direction of that remuda. His purpose was evidently to help the chousers corral the horses.

Dust filtered across the yard, its scent tangy. Colonel Hardin, in a grey hat with a turned-down brim, and a short-tailed riding coat, came down to the porch steps, finally, and looked hawkishly at the lawman tying up out there.

'You escorted Lon home?' he asked. 'I didn't know you gave them that kind of service, Will.'

Chance smiled. 'I usually don't, Colonel.'

'Why this time, then?'

'Well; just to sort of explain that he didn't do anything really.'

'I know that. Two of my men told me that at breakfast this morning. They said you singled out Ox-Yoke to persecute us.'

Will was chagrined. 'You know better than that, Colonel.'

'Then why did you lock him up?'

'Well; there is a town ordinance, and if he hadn't been so darned out in the open with it, I wouldn't have hauled him, but there he was for everyone to see, standing right in front of me ... You understand?'

Hardin was not that interested. 'What kind of shape is he in?'

'Fine this morning. I pumped a gallon of black java into him last night. This morning he's rearing to go.'

Hardin's tough eyes hardened. 'He'd better be rearing to go—or damned if he won't go in a different direction. Down the road!'

Will leaned to watch the loose-stock get wheeled and turned until the entire remuda without a single cut-back swung through the big gate of a circular pole corral. 'Got a gather coming up?' he asked.

'First thing in the morning,' replied Colonel Hardin, also watching the experts out there working his horses. 'I've got a right fine crew this season, Will.' Hardin was no longer

70

concerned about Lon Stearn. He turned his head. 'Care to look at some good horses?'

Will answered honestly as he pulled upright off the rack. 'Colonel, there is nothing I'd rather look at.'

They walked out there, smelled the tangy dust and the sweat of many horses, then hooked booted feet upon a corral stringer as the riders turned towards the barn, leading their saddle-mounts after someone had swung and latched the corral gate.

Hardin looked intently at all those horses of his. Will Chance was looking just as intently at the cowboys. There perhaps should have been a man there in dark trousers and a dark hat. There wasn't; every cowboy out there Will had seen in town a number of times before the coach robbery.

'That big *grulla*,' stated the colonel, as though he and Will were both admiring the horses, 'is tough and rough-riding and mean, but you know, Will, I can't quite make myself get rid of him. He's got spirit and courage.'

Will looked for a blue gelding, found him, made an assessment, and offered his two-bits worth. 'He's got an ugly head, Colonel.'

George Hardin was one of those men who would not defend cattle from denigration, but his horses and his riders he would defend instantly. He looked sulphurously at Will. 'I've seen a damned sight prettier town constables, too. What's that got to do with a horse being spirited and brave?'

'Mean little eyes,' stated Will, deliberately antagonising the older man. 'Bad disposition, Colonel, and anyway he's too long-legged to be a good ropehorse.'

Hardin was red in the face. 'Whoever told you you were qualified to pass any judgements on my horses? That just happens to be one of the best stockhorses on the place—except that you can't trust him.'

Will was still looking at the horses when he hauled back and turned in the direction of the barn. 'Lon told me you had your best animals stalled, Colonel. I've seen your worst now I'd like to see your best.'

Will did not hesitate nor did he glance over a shoulder to see whether or not George Hardin was trailing after him. The colonel was, apparently not because he cared about going over to the barn but rather because, angered and articulate, he had something more to tell that lawman from town.

There were four horsemen just leaving the barn, having freed their saddle-animals and having draped their gear from the saddle-pole. They stared with interest and curiosity at the town marshal, and nodded. Only one of them looked mildly antagonistic. That was Lon Stearn.

They trooped on out of the barn heading across the yard. This was their day to loaf, to play poker, to do their laundry or to lope over to town if they cared to.

There were horse-stalls on either side of a very wide earthen runway in the horse-barn. The old log structure smelled pleasantly of horses, and hay in the loft. It was cool and shady.

Colonel Hardin watched Will pause before several stalls gazing in. At the stall where the Ox-Yoke remount stallion stood calmly, Hardin said, 'That's the foundation of Ox-Yoke saddle-stock. Now let me hear you fault *him!*'

Will smiled at the handsome, big muscular stallion, 'Couldn't fault him, Colonel. No better stock on earth than Morgans.'

Hardin was not entirely ameliorated but he seemed not to have quite as many ruffled feathers as he went closer to lean and also admire the stallion. 'He's sired every top horse we've worked on Ox-Yoke for the past seven years. He don't look that old, does he?'

Will agreed that the stallion certainly did not look that old, while at the same time his eyes were swinging farther along in the gloom until he made out the large black horse which had prompted him to come to the barn in the fast place.

He walked down there, the colonel trailed along, the black horse came over to nuzzle the lawman, and Colonel Hardin watched stonily without uttering a word about the black gelding.

Will leaned in studying the horse. Particularly, he was interested in the animal's shoes which he could not see because of the straw bedding.

'This one isn't out of that Morgan stud,' he stated.

Hardin grudgingly agreed. 'No. Too much standard-bred in him to pass as Morgan.'

'Your horse?' Will asked, and got another of those grudging nods.

'Yes.'

'Got a bad tendon,' stated Will.

Hardin slowly straightened up stiffly to his full height, angered again. 'What the hell are you talking about?' he demanded, and reached to unlatch the stall door. 'That horse is as sound as new money. Will, you never struck me as an obnoxious feller before.'

Will edged in ahead of the colonel, laid a light hand upon the black horse's shoulder, eased it steadily down as far as the strong, sound tendon, then squeezed for the horse to lift his foot. He obliged. Will scraped out the bedding and saw the city-head horseshoe nails and the journeyman-blacksmithing job on the shoe.

He lowered the leg as he straightened up patting the horse as he said, 'I was wrong, Colonel. It must have been the shadows in here but it looked to me from outside the stall that he had the start of a pair of bowed tendons.'

Hardin closed the door with monumental disdain and dusted off his hands. 'You don't know up from down about horses,' he averred.

Will agreed imperturbably. 'You just might be right at that, Colonel. Well; I got to get back to town. Thanks for your time.'

Will crossed to the rack over in front of the main-house to get his animal, swung over leather, threw a careless wave in the direction of the barn, and also in the direction of the bunkhouse where Waite Culpepper was standing, thumbs in his bulletbelt, stoically watching as Will Chance left the Ox-Yoke yard. Neither Colonel Hardin at the barn nor his rangeboss at the log bunk-house waved back.

Waite eventually ambled down to the barn-opening where George Hardin was standing. 'He picked on Lon,' stated Culpepper. 'All the fellers in the bunk-house agree to that.'

Hardin growled his retort. 'I always liked him. But this morning he turned out to be a smart-alec. I never noticed that in him before, Waite.'

Culpepper, who had little use for any townsmen, was willing to augment his employer's annoyance. 'He's always been a little big for his britches, Colonel.'

A mile out Will Chance eased over into a long-legged lope heading south-easterly in the direction of town. By now those respectable folks in town were sitting down to their Sunday roast, or leg of lamb with mint jelly, still wearing their Sunday-go-to-meeting clothing.

Except for a few men who tended to congregate apart from the respectable folks over at the poolhall which was next door to the locked-up general store, Sunday was a day given over to reverence and rest in Morganton, and also to eating.

It was the eating Constable Chance was thinking about when he finally had Morganton in sight with the sun slanting away over his right shoulder. He probably would have been invited to share the noonday meal at Ox-Yoke if he hadn't aroused so much hostility back there.

CHAPTER NINE

THE PLAN

Dan Cowper was notified by the blacksmith, Morgan, and Will himself visited Herlihy's saloon to tell the barman they would all meet this evening at the jailhouse office.

With that settled Will went to the cafe for something to eat, and while he was down there Charley Graham the retired stage driver who owned the telegraph franchise for Morgan Valley, came in looking for the lawman. Charley had a telegram which he delivered personally, then stood a moment dolorously eyeing Will.

'You're stirring up a hell of a mess,' he said.

Will thumbed back his hat. 'Charley, do you fellers take some kind of an oath to keep things confidential that cross your desk?'

The older man nodded. 'Yes. But I ain't telling anyone else—just you. A man in my fix, Will, has got to read what he's receiving over the telegraph key, you realise.' Charley jutted his wedge-shaped jaw at the mustard-coloured slip of folded paper he had just de-livered. 'You're going to stir up trouble with that answer to your telegram to the War Department.'

Will said nothing. For a longer moment they gazed steadily at one another then Charley Graham turned on his heel.

Will straightened around at the counter, opened the folded paper and read its contents—twice—then he pocketed it, finished his meal and afterwards walked out into the shadowy late afternoon, heading for the jailhouse upon the opposite side of the road.

Sunday was just about over with and finished. So were all those inhibiting restrictions which people could feel righteous about, for just so long.

Herlihy's place had more than just a few of the ordinarily irreverent rangeriders lined along the bar and scattered among the tables, drinking leisurely pitchers of beer. The

77

townsmen were there in considerable numbers. Mostly they were still dressed in their Sunday attire, but a few had even gone so far as to change back into their more comfortable work-a-day clothing. It was hard to truly enjoy beer in a tight little celluloid collar.

Dan Herlihy was swabbing the bartop when the apothecary strolled in and found a place at the bar. Herlihy drew a beer, skived off excess foam with a stiff forefinger and went down to set up the glass in front of Cowper.

'You heard we're to meet across the road after supper?' he asked, and Cowper reached for the beer before nodding his head.

'Reg told me.'

They both looked around but the blacksmith was not in sight. Herlihy leaned over to softly say, 'Will was out at Ox-Yoke today. Look up near the free-lunch counter: That's Waite Culpepper and one of the Ox-Yoke crew up there.'

Cowper did not look, nor did he especially like this conspiratorial attitude of Dan's, so he hoisted his glass and kept drinking until someone farther away banged on the bartop and Herlihy had to depart.

Cowper finished that beer, bought a cigar from Herlihy and went out front into the gloaming to light up. He was like most men in Morgan Valley; he liked cigars but could not afford them very often. Usually, he only bought one upon some kind of special occasion. There was no such occasion today—that he knew of anyway—but this evening the apothecary-undertaker just simply felt like being a wastrel.

Later, when he headed for the lighted jailhouse office, he had to reluctantly pitch away the cigar. It was getting so short it was a hazard to the tip of his nose.

Dan Cowper was the first one to arrive at the meeting. Will Chance had made a pot of coffee on his office wood-stove and was sampling a cup when Cowper arrived. He too had a cup.

Later, when all four of them were there, and nightfall had become an accomplished fact outside, Will went to his desk with his coffee cup, picked up the mustard-coloured slip of paper he had received at the cafe, and offered it to Cowper first. The others waited in silence while the apothecary read the paper. Will was rolling a smoke when Cowper screwed up his face and said, 'I didn't know that.'

Will gestured for the undertaker to hand the telegram to Reg, then he lit up and sat down behind the desk. Reg looked surprised too, but he said nothing. He handed the paper to Herlihy, then Reg faced Will with a caustic look on his face. 'How'd you come to get that message?' he asked.

Will's reply was brief. 'A hunch I had,' he said, and leaned to accept back the slip of paper as Herlihy passed it over. 'Hardin's a widower. I knew that. I was just sort of curious about the rest of it, and there is the answer. He had a son born shortly after the war. Well; I been out to Ox-Yoke a hundred times over the years and I never saw a son out there. I've had long visits with the colonel a lot of times, too, and he never once mentioned having children—having a son.'

The blacksmith held up a hand. 'Wait a minute. Let's get to the nubbin' of this, Will. Are we talkin' about old Hardin having a son who is a stage robber?'

'We're talking about old Hardin having a guest at the main-house,' replied the lawman. 'His guest arrived the same day as the robbery. His guest was riding a big breedy black horse. Today I went out there and looked at the horse and at his shoes. City-head nails and town shoes. *That's* what we're talking about, Reg. Whether this is Colonel Hardin's son or not I don't know. I *do* know he lied to me when I asked about that black horse, and I also figure he would have told a bigger lie if I'd asked him point-blank if there was anyone in the house.'

Herlihy was standing at the stove refilling a cup when Will stopped speaking. He turned towards the others to say something. 'Well, what's the answer fellers? To me it looks like we just opened a box of rattlesnakes. If that son of a bitch was the old man's flesh-an'-

80

blood son, and he robbed Henry Devereaux's stage, and the colonel is hiding him, the rest of it's obvious enough. Someone's got to fetch him to town and lock him up for trial, don't they?'

Before Will could reply Dan Cowper made a dry comment, 'You think Colonel Hardin is going to sit back and watch someone do that?' he asked the saloonman. 'If you do, I'd like to have you standing in front of me, out there . . . And he can count on Waite Culpepper. More'n likely he can count on those four range-riders of his as well.'

Herlihy did not give an inch. 'Don't make a damn bit of difference,' he told the apothecary with a truculent look on his face. 'He could be General Grant and he'd still have to face the law. Maybe they got two kinds of law in the East, but out here by gawd we got just one kind and it fits everyone, stage robbers or ex-Secesh-colonels, or big cowman or whatever.'

Reg looked disconsolately at Dan Herlihy. 'You missed your calling. You should have been a Congressman.' As usual Reg's dourness dampened the others. In this instance it ended the budding dispute between the saloonman and the apothecary. 'We don't have to storm out there like Custer did, anyway. If we did that Cowper's right—we'd probably run into about the same thing Custer got.'

'Well, the colonel and his highwayman aren't going to oblige us by ridin' into town,' said Herlihy with dripping sarcasm.

Morgan was unaffected. 'They won't have to,' he replied. 'I spent a full day out at the creek with my spyglass and I learnt a little about the habits of Ox-Yoke while I was fightin' flies and mosquitoes . . . For instance, Waite parcels out the day's work right early, and when those riders finish breakfast they and Waite saddle up and ride out. That leaves the cook, Colonel Hardin, and whoever else he's got at the house with him. Three men.'

'Three guns,' growled Herlihy.

Reg pierced the saloonman with a look. 'How would you like to shut your damned mouth until I'm finished,' he exclaimed, and did not await an answer. 'There is a way to get up behind the cookshack out there while keeping its rear wall between a feller and the rest of the yard. I studied that over while I was at the creek. I can show you how to do it. Only trouble would be if the cook came walking around back for some reason while someone was sneakin' up there. But I don't think that'd happen. He never came around back all the while I was watching the yard. Okay; that would eliminate the cook—and his gun— wouldn't it? Then all we'd have to do would be sneak around the mainhouse.'

Will, who had said almost nothing since the conference had begun, now made a suggestion. 'It's a good plan. Someone had ought to ride out a ways though and keep an eye on Waite and the other Ox-Yoke riders. It could be darned embarrassing if they came back for some reason, or if they were within hearing distance and we had to use guns.'

Reg shrugged that off. 'All right. One of us can ride out and spy on the Ox-Yoke crew.' He looked at Dan Herlihy. 'What other darned objections do you have?'

Herlihy flushed. 'I'd like it if you'd be the one to ride out,' he snapped, and Reg Morgan imperturbably nodded his head. 'All right. I'll ride out.' He turned. 'Will . . . ?'

Morgan's clear meaning had to do with when they would put their plan into action. Will, as lawman and chief-schemer had the final say.

'Tomorrow morning?' he suggested. 'Leave town before sunup and get out there along the creek before daylight?'

The others found no fault with that. At least none of them offered a different scheme, although Herlihy said, 'Fetch carbines as well as beltguns—just in case.' Then, as he sipped coffee another idea arrived and he also said, 'If there is trouble and Culpepper fetches back the riding crew we're going to be in trouble up to our armpits. Hell! there's not a one of us got any real right going up against the kind of gun-handy riders old Hardin hires . . . Will; maybe we'd ought to recruit another four or five fellers.'

Reg snorted. 'You go riding out there even

in the dark lookin' like a blasted army, Dan, and there won't be any way for us to get up close without being discovered.'

This was the second time Morgan had cut the ground from beneath the saloonman and Herlihy was an individual without endless patience. He leaned to set aside his cup and started to square around to face the blacksmith when Cowper casually strolled towards the stove to get some coffee for himself and halted squarely between the saloonman and the blacksmith. Cowper spoke over their heads towards Will at the desk.

'Four *good* men are worth more than maybe ten men who are just sort of mediocre, aren't they?'

Will knew exactly what Cowper was doing. 'Yeah, I'd say,' he agreed, and looked at Herlihy. 'Well, do we go as four good men who can work together or do we round up a penny-ante army and go like that?'

'I'll tell you where Reg Morgan can go,' growled the saloonman, and they all laughed except Reg, he only smiled, but that was the same in Reg Morgan as raucous hilarity in anyone else.

The moment passed. They all got more coffee, drank it standing around saying little, and afterwards they trooped out into the night bound for home and as much sleep as they could get.

Will lingered there to close down the

damper on his wood-stove, sink their coffee cups in the bucket of water beside the stove, blow down the lamp-mantle to plunge the jailhouse into darkness, and to finally exit as far as the plankwalk where he locked the place from outside and turned to make a slow survey of his town.

It was as quiet and orderly as it was supposed to be. The effects of a fine Sabbath wore off quickly enough but usually they were able to cling doggedly at least until the end of an orderly Sunday.

Will rolled a smoke, studied doorways as he lit up and strolled in the direction of the rooming-house, and smiled to himself over the abrasive sentiments displayed between Herlihy and Morgan. They were both good men. Their dispute wouldn't have amounted to anything. There were times when Reg could test the patience of a saint. Tonight had been one of them.

There was still a little commotion at the saloon, but not an appreciable lot of it and otherwise the town, up and down its main wide, dusty thoroughfare anyway, was quiet and empty and drowsily dark the way Will Chance liked to see his town this time of night, because it meant he could go straight home and to bed, which is what he did this night.

Elsewhere, a couple of his friends got out their guns and solemnly examined them. None of these men with the exception of Will, were experienced gunhands. Maybe they had once been years ago, but none of them had maintained that warlike distinction since those bloody early days.

CHAPTER TEN

MANHUNT!

About the only actual certainty which accompanies springtime is the uncertainty of its weather. Some mornings are wonderfully bland and warm, like midsummer mornings. Other mornings are as cold as winter and this particular morning was one of the latter.

They stood around out back of the jailhouse blowing on their hands and saying not a word amongst themselves, bundled in coats and gloves and mufflers, looking as morose as they had every right to look.

None of them, with the possible exception of Will Chance, had had to arise this early and go out into the cold for many years. They all had indoor jobs except Will, and any morning of the week Reg Morgan had his backsides set towards a glowing forge. As they finally got astride heading northward up the back-alley, he said, 'Gawddammit; why do sensible merchants and businessmen from town get tangled up in situations like this—anyway!'

No one answered.

The town was warmly snug and silently slumbering. Their hoof falls made a rattling echo. There were no lights along either side of the alleyway and over on Main Street the only two establishments which kept lanterns alight all night long were the liverybarn at the lower end of town, and the church-porch at the other end of town.

Several drowsy dogs felt a moral obligation to rouse themselves from tow-sack beds in wagon-sheds or on rear porches to raise up and growl, then bark as the wraith-like possemen rode past. These sounds echoed throughout town. No one came to peer out a window; at least none of the riders saw anyone watching their departure from town.

Will led. He cut westerly up where the alleyway intersected with an ancient wagon-road which came into Morganton from the far rangeland in the distant west. Very few people used this old road any longer. Its original purpose had been to offer access to the settlement to buffalo hunters and traders. Since those distant days the road had been straightened and established so that it bisected town from the south to the north, and the old-time road had been completely abandoned.

For Will, there was nothing unpleasant about what he was embarked upon. At least not yet. And as for the chill, he was bundled against it, and was more or less accustomed to it in any event.

He did not consider the weather, he thought instead of what they were going to do when they got out at least as far as the creek.

He smoked and patiently plodded along unmindful of the hunched-up sullen lumps riding behind him. Once they spooked a band of someone's saddle-stock and all that sudden snorting, whistling, then wild running, got their own animals fired up.

This brought comment. Herlihy told his mount its parents hadn't been wedded at its inception. Reg Morgan told his animal its mother was a female dog, and Dan Cowper took the only rational approach, instead of swearing at his own fractious mount he eloquently swore at the fleeing loose-stock.

They all immediately felt better.

Except for this one interlude the ride out as far as the creek was uneventful—just cold.

When they reached the sooty silhouettes along the creek and dismounted to lead their homes in among them, they started up some game, either deer or antelope it was impossible to tell which, but this swift exodus of animals around them did not excite their saddle-stock at all. For one thing the animals had now been ridden far enough to have most of the giddiness worked out, and for another thing the much lighter animals did not make nearly as much noise in flight as a band of horses made.

Reg Morgan surprised everyone by producing, along with his brass spyglass, a quart of brandy-laced black coffee which he had carried in a sack-wrapped glass bottle.

The coffee was still hot. They all drank, shook their heads over Morgan's thoughtfulness as though they simply could not believe he had really done this, then they mellowed a little and had another swallow or two apiece, and continued to get mellow until they had drained the bottle. Reg hung it from a high limb among the creek-willows and started to roll a smoke.

They had about an hour to kill, judging from the look of the far horizon. There was not even a thin blue wedge yet to separate the crust of the world from the higher gloom of the shrouded dark night.

Tobacco smoke smelled good in the thin cold air. They were warm inside and out. There actually was little to complain about. Herlihy wondered if it might not be a good idea for them to tie the horses at the creek and, taking fullest advantage of this darkness, sneak up to the Ox-Yoke buildings now.

Will did not think so and Reg agreed with that by saying someone over there might cut loose and one of them could perhaps get injured. Anyway, their scheme was not to risk discovery before the riding crew pulled out.

Herlihy looked at Dan Cowper and shrugged. Cowper smiled and whittled off a chew of plug-cut, pouched it and stoically stood there, head pulled down half way into his blanket coat for all the world like an erect turtle.

Dawn came slowly, almost grudgingly, and the cold lingered. If there was any change at all it got colder between first-light and sunrise, a period of about an hour and a half, but the men did not suffer and neither did their livestock because, uniquely enough, it did not appreciably change for the worse down along the creek.

Eventually they could make out the ranch buildings. Even before they could make that distinction though they had seen a light come on in the cookshack and moments later they smelled wood-smoke.

It was while they were standing loosely there, in among the concealing willows and their shadows, that Reg Morgan wrinkled his face and said, 'You fellers smell that coffee?'

They didn't smell it and they did not believe he smelt it either but no one commented.

A low-toned little bell rang twice. By that time, though, it was possible to smell more than boiling coffee, they could also smell meat frying. No one commented on what everyone's reaction to these aromas was. No one had to comment.

Finally, Herlihy said, 'Won't be long now,' and he was correct. About ten minutes later with the daylight turning a lighter shade of gun-metalstain, men trooped from the cookshack, milled a little out in the yard for their after-breakfast smoke, then ambled off in the direction of the log horse-barn, clearly visible to the men back in among the creek willows, but most noticeable to Will Chance who was using Morgan's telescoping spy-glass.

He handed the thing around. When Herlihy finished with it he said, 'Reg, you are supposed to shag them, remember. Now don't get too darned close, will you?' Instead of an answer Herlihy got a look of monumental disdain.

The riders took their time. For one thing they were required by unwritten range law never to enter anyone's barn with a lighted cigarette. For another thing, they were buttoning up against the chill and standing there looking all around for a moment or two before trampling out the smokes and heading on down inside the dark old barn.

Cowper shook his head. 'I never before knew cowboys wasted so much time getting started for the day.'

Reg made a slightly defensive comment about that. 'It's cold. A man'd just as soon put off setting his behind on cold leather as long as he can.'

The riders eventually came forth, turned northward and started out of the yard together—then one man's horse suddenly bogged his head and bucked as hard as he could. Evidently someone else didn't care for ice-cold leather against their hide so early in the morning. The cowboy rode hard, putting up a valiant fight to stay aboard.

With an excuse to forget their own chilliness the other Ox-Yoke men whooped and called out profane encouragement.

The cowboy finally fought his horse's head up, the bucking stopped, and the angry rider sank in his hooks to the chap-guards. The horse gave a loud snort, bunched all four legs under him and sprang ahead without touching ground for twelve feet, and he lit running.

The other men laughed. That sound carried easily and pleasantly out to the distant men at the creek.

Cowper chuckled in appreciation. He and the men with him at the creek had understood every aspect of what had just happened over there at the north end of Ox-Yoke's yard.

Will lowered the spyglass. 'That's the lot,' he reported. 'The cook, Hardin and the highwayman are all that's left.'

Reg Morgan said, 'I been thinkin'. Suppose Herlihy and I skulk forward now and grab the cook. Two men could maybe do that better than—'

'You,' exclaimed the saloonman, levelling a stiff forefinger, 'are supposed to get astride and shag those darned cowboys and make sure they don't just make a big sashay and head back here.'

Reg considered. 'How do I know you fellers

will be able to sidle over there without being caught at it?'

Herlihy groaned loudly and rolled up his eyes. 'Now we got the only feller in the world who knows how to sneak up onto a cookshack that don't have any windows in the back wall . . . Where were you when Colonel Custer needed someone like you, Reg?'

'You can go to hell,' said Morgan, and turned to run a thumb under the cinch of his rig before climbing aboard to follow the Ox-Yoke riders. As he was reining away to pass northward just beyond the willows he looked back and said, 'Don't blame me, now, if you fellers mess this all up.'

Will and Dan Cowper exchanged a wry look without speaking, and Herlihy would have said something no doubt except that by the time he was ready to speak Reg was on up through the willows too far. Herlihy would have had to raise his voice and that was something none of them wanted to do.

They watched the Ox-Yoke men for a while then turned and also watched Reg Morgan, who was discreetly keeping the creek and its willows between himself and the yonder rangeriders.

While this was happening a thin streamer of sunlight finally arrived and Will put his forward attention upon the distant peaks where the sun was rising. As yet, there were only those golden streamers, but there was a

93

magnificent glow like a molten halo out beyond that farthest peak, meaning that sunrise was only a short while away.

Will turned, studied the buildings, studied those distant riders, and decided they had better begin their forward stalk while there were still enough shadows up along the intervening open country, between the creek and the back of the log cookshack, to aid them.

He looked around. Herlihy and Cowper were watching him and ignoring everything else. They knew exactly what his thoughts were. All he had to do was jerk his head.

They secured their horses, brought out their saddle-guns and when Will ploughed through the icy creek they both followed after him. Out through the willows on the west bank it was easier to study the buildings. Clearly, what Reg had observed was that, since there was no rear-wall window in the cookshack, as long as the stalkers kept that blind wall between them and the buildings around front and upon the far side of the big ranchyard, they could get over at least as far as the cookshack without difficulty.

Dan Cowper raised a gloved right hand to point the way. 'Like Reg said, if someone don't accidentally walk around there—hell—we can make it without difficulty.'

They struck out of their cover and immediately felt just as exposed as they definitely were. Not a word was spoken from this point on, although actually if the cook or perhaps even the colonel had seen them, had recognised each one of them, it would have been more embarrassing than dangerous. George Hardin had known each one of them for years. He wouldn't have started shooting, he would just have stood there, hands on hips, calling them by name, and nothing would have been as humiliating as trying to act like stalking manhunters only to be discovered by someone who never thought of them as anything but a blacksmith, an apothecary-undertaker, and a town constable.

But they made it without being discovered. They got completely across the intervening distance and reached the back wall of the cookshack just as the sun finally came jumping up from behind that far-away peak as though it were the pip being squeezed from an olive.

Golden brilliance flooded outward and downward in all directions. It was still cold but it would not be cold very much longer.

CHAPTER ELEVEN

'DON'T MOVE!'

Some men can work perfectly together. Cowper and Herlihy flattened along the log wall waiting for Will to decide their next move, and Will did not keep them in suspense very long.

'I'll go around the north side,' he explained. 'You boys slip along here until you've got the main-house in sight. Watch it close, because I can't enter the cookshack without going around to the front porch, and if anyone is watching from the main-house they're going to see me sure as the devil.'

Neither Herlihy nor Cowper asked what they were to do in the event that Will were discovered entering the cookshack, they just nodded, then allowed him to move out first, before they went down to the south corner of the building.

For Will, the danger was still more one of discovery than of physical violence. Colonel Hardin would recognise him even from behind. What Colonel Hardin was certainly going to be interested in was the fact that Constable Chance had arrived on foot in his yard, with a Winchester in his hand and with his coat unbuttoned and hauled back on the right side to expose his Colt-handle.

There was nothing to be done about this except hope the colonel was not gazing out a front window into the ranchyard just yet.

Will paused at the corner out front, looked both ways, saw nothing to upset him, heard the cook singing in very bad border-Spanish about his lost love, took one big forward step and

96

reached the porch. He could not conceal his approach from here on. He was booted and spurred but even if he had arrived barefoot or in moccasins, the porch planking groaned under his weight so he moved very swiftly as far as the doorway, reached with a gloved hand to haul the door back and to swing up his Winchester with the other gloved hand.

For a moment the cook went on with his terrible singing while he draped two soggy flour-sack dish towels from a wire stretched behind the cook stove, then he turned. His song died away, his hand continued to hang in the air at the wire, and his pale eyes slowly puckered and drew out into a narrow stare as he said, 'Marshal; what in the hell are you fixing to do with that gun? The colonel's got a rule around here about folks pointing guns and . . .'

Will said, 'Shut up, will you!' and moved into the big room with its long table, its benches and cupboards and its heat and fragrances. The cook was alone. He was also watching everything Will did as though he did not really believe any of it could be happening.

Will knew the cook very well. Most folks in Morgan Valley knew him. He was the cousin of the other old rangerider in town who owned the telegraph franchise. The telegrapher's name was Charley Graham and the name of the Ox-Yoke's cook was Wright Graham. Wright was a few years younger than Charley, and when they had both got too old to roll out on the black, below-zero winter mornings to go hunt snow-blinded cattle, Charley had headed for town but his cousin had refused to leave the range.

Now, he said, 'Marshal, darn it all, I got to get the colonel's breakfast you know. I'd appreciate it if you'd tell me . . .' The words trailed off as Dan Herlihy and the other Dan, Dan Cowper, came in by the same doorway also with saddleguns in hand.

Wright Graham stepped to a bench and sank down, his paunch easing comfortably out and over his belt as he watched those three armed men. He looked longest at Cowper, whom he knew as the pill-roller and undertaker from town. He had never before seen either the undertaker or the saloonman bundled, hatted, and heavily armed.

'You fellers up to something,' he asked plaintively. 'You playin' some sort of silly game?'

Will gestured towards a front window. Herlihy strolled over. Will went over by the table, cocked up a leg and asked if Wright Graham always got the colonel's breakfast this late, after the riders had departed.

Graham raised and dropped thick, beefy shoulders. 'I do like I'm told to do,' he retorted. 'That's exactly what I do. Listen, Will, you're going to get the colonel mad as a wet hen, doing stuff like this.'

'When you've cooked his breakfast the past couple of days,' persisted the lawman, 'have you prepared just one meal?'

The cook began to look pained. 'There is only one colonel ain't there?' he asked. 'Will; if you boys want to sidle back out of here I'll never say a word.'

Herlihy made a low whistle from the window, then turned. 'Hardin's coming,' he reported, and gazed without trepidation at Will.

Cowper said, 'Alone?' and the cook started to arise and to turn angry at the same time. 'What the hell do you mean—alone? Of course he'll be alone. Listen to me, you fellers—'

Will pushed his carbine barrel gently into the folds of flesh around the cook's middle, pushed a little harder until Wright Graham sank back down upon his bench looking helpless, red-necked, and irritably baffled.

Will stepped back. 'You boys keep an eye on this one and the colonel. Now that we've got them separated I'll go see about nailing the one in the house.'

Colonel Hardin trooped up onto the yonder porch, his footsteps solidly sounding. As he reached the door and raised a hand to push on through the cook opened his mouth to bleat, to make some kind of warning sound anyway, and Herlihy moved swiftly, sank a powerful set of talons into the cook's fleshy shoulder with his left hand and pushed his gunbarrel into the cook's side with his right hand. The cook hung there, grimacing but not uttering a sound.

Colonel Hardin walked in, and stopped dead still in his tracks, eyes very slowly moving from gun to gun and from man to man.

Will stepped back around to get between the colonel and the doorway. He got into position none too quickly because George Hardin, age notwithstanding, was a much quicker man to react than his cook had been. He swung on the balls of his feet to lunge back out of the cookshack.

Will shoved the saddlegun-barrel forward and blocked the doorway with his body. Hardin grudgingly and very slowly lost his tenseness and his thrusting momentum. So far not a word had been spoken. Now, the cook said, 'Colonel, I tried to yell a warning.'

Hardin stepped back ignoring his cook and looked at only one man: Will Chance. 'What are you doing here?' he asked roughly. 'What are all *three* of you doing here?'

Will did not answer. He gestured the colonel away from the door with his saddlegun, then Dan Herlihy moved over, reached to settle a powerful grip upon the colonel's shoulder and roughly yank the older man back and away.

Hardin reacted with a savage lunge at the saloonman but that was also blocked, this time by the apothecary. Hardin subsided, and turned again to face the constable, but Will was already moving out of the building. Hardin called his name and Will kept right on moving.

He leaned his carbine at the corner of the porch, and stood in overhang-shadows for a while studying the main-house, while behind him inside the cookshack Colonel Hardin finally began to speak.

Will moved farther along the front of the porch, dropped over the far side and went back around to the rear of the cookshack. He could hear the fierce argument going on inside. Another time that might have amused him. Right now he did not listen to it.

In order to reach the main-house he had to pass between three outbuildings: the cookshack, the smoke-house, and the more distant and much larger combination shoeing-shed and wagon-shed.

After that he had roughly two hundred feet to cross which was also exposed, before he could get up close to the east wall of the main-house.

If the highwayman did not nail him at any one of those exposed places, his chances of at least reaching the house were excellent.

He made the first crossing from the rear of the cookshack to the rear of the smoke-house without any difficulty. He leaned at the corner of the smaller, thick-walled building for a long while studying the house.

There was no sign of activity of any kind

over there. The sun was climbing, the yard was crystal-clear in all directions, and a seeming great hush overhung everything—or maybe that was Will's imagination.

He started to make his second crossing, the one from the smoke-house over to the rear wall of the combination wagon- and shoeing-shed. He was mid-way when a door slammed over at the main-house. The noise acted on Will Chance as though it had been an electrified prod. He jumped the last dozen or so feet and lit over there behind the large log shed with his right hand lightly resting upon a walnut gunstock.

But that was all that happened; someone over there had slammed a door. He peered from around the corner, saw nothing, waited a long while for another sound or perhaps movement, and in the end decided he was not going to locate either, and began measuring the last long crossing he had to make to reach the east side of the main-house.

Since there was not a breath of air stirring, what that closed door signified was that there was indeed someone over at the main-house, but although that might have clarified a doubtful issue for someone, it did nothing more than buttress Will Chance's conviction. He had not doubted there was someone at the main-house for a long while now.

Something else that sound did, though, was heighten his caution. Whoever that was across

102

the yard from him was up and stirring and presumably armed and capable.

That couple of hundred feet began to look more like a country mile.

He waited, trying to imagine that highwayman at the house, trying to surmise what he might be doing. It put a considerable strain on things, not knowing the highwayman, having no way at all of guessing where he would be and what he might be up to at the time Will made his dash.

In the end he did the only thing he could do, he took down a deep breath and sprang out into the open, running as hard as he could, hoping with all his heart that the outlaw would not just happen to glance from a window and see him running like that.

Nothing happened except that a noisy old bluejay in a tree near the house squawked his head off at the sight of the running two-legged thing down below. He continued to scold even after Will was against the house-wall breathing as though he had run three or four times as far.

The bird was evidently a ranchyard mascot, or was at least tolerated in the treetops around the home-place. If the men had not been tolerant of him they would have blown him to Kingdom Come long ago.

The bird seemed especially intolerant of strangers. How he knew Will was not a member of the riding crew was anyone's guess, but he seemed to know, and furthermore he stayed with Will, hopping from tree-limb to tree-limb as he scolded.

Anything as insignificant as a bird at a time like this would normally have been ignored, but that bluejay kept up his shrill scolding and indubitably it was going to draw someone's attention.

Will looked up, located the bird without trouble and wished he dared shoot the blasted creature.

Then someone coming out onto the porch around front diverted Will but did not divert the bluejay. Will heard the boot-steps coming slowly along the porch towards the eastern corner. Evidently whoever that was around front was looking in the treetops as they walked trying to find the bird in order to locate the reason for his agitation.

Will's lethal anger at the bird was sublimated while he carefully drew his Colt, flattened and waited. There was one aspect of this matter which was favourable. He was now going to be able to get the drop on the colonel's house-guest and that, at least, resolved the issue of how Will was going to affect the confrontation he had been heading for ever since he and his possemen had ridden out from town.

The oncoming boot-steps seemed to slow almost to a halt at the corner. Will raised his Colt, held his breath, and when the boot-steps picked up again and came right up to the corner, Will finally cocked his sixgun.

The stranger moved into view dressed in black trousers, dark shirt and black boots.

Will said, 'Don't move! Not one damned move!' The stranger turned to stone, then very gently turned, just from the neck up.

Will was looking into the large violet eyes of a very handsome taffy-haired girl!

CHAPTER TWELVE

THE WOMAN

She stared at Will Chance as though she could not believe her eyes, stared at his cocked weapon, the badge on his shirtfront visible through his opened jacket, then finally overcame her pure astonishment and relaxed a little as she continued to obey his terse order not to move.

For Will, who had been expecting someone at least as lethal as Ladd Denton, the notorious outlaw of the south-desert country, that lithe, handsome woman up there came as a complete jolt. She was unarmed but there were indications that she had often enough worn a bullet belt and a holstered weapon.

He lowered his Colt but did not ease off the hammer. 'Who else is inside?' he demanded of her.

She almost sighed as she replied. 'No one.'

He had his doubts simply because he had expected a renegade and all he had now was a lovely woman with very dark blue eyes and taffy hair that caught vagrant sunbeams and held them.

'Stand where you are,' he said, and reached for the railing to vault up onto the porch, then he gestured 'Turn back; walk to the door and open it, then step to one side.'

She went through the entire routine precisely as he had ordered her to, and at the door when she turned she said, 'He's not in there, Marshal. There is no one in there.'

Will looked steadily at her. 'Who's not in there?'

'My husband.'

'And who is your husband?'

'Ladd Denton,' she said softly. 'He's not here.'

Will considered, then gestured for her to precede him, not as a shield but because he did not want her at his back unwatched. She led the way from room to room as though willing to demonstrate that what she had said on the porch was the truth.

Evidently it was. They found no-one, and in fact in the kitchen there was evidence to indicate that only two people had eaten at the small table. He finally told her to sit. She went to a chair at the table, sat down and looked at

106

him as though she were about to patiently endure something she was quite familiar with. She said, 'He is not here, Marshal, and that is all I'm going to tell you.'

Will went to a window, glanced in the direction of the cookshack, glanced farther out, over the distant, heat-hazed rangeland, saw an individual horseman coming almost indolently towards the yard, guessed that this would be Reg Morgan, and after a moment of watching, turned to face the handsome woman.

'Was your husband here?' he asked.

She shrugged. 'Marshal, I told you—I've said all I'm going to say. He is not here.'

'But he was here,' stated Will. 'He robbed that coach north of town.'

She looked at him as though he were some kind of mildly interesting peculiarity. She was not hostile, nor rude, nor hard and defiant, she was just herself; calm and polite and pig-headed.

He turned to look out yonder at the approaching rider again. It had never occurred to him that this might be Ladd Denton. Nor was it, although perhaps some other lawman would have expected it to be Denton. It was in fact Reg Morgan, exactly as Will had expected that it would be.

He faced the woman again. She could see the horseman through the same window. She shook her head. 'Sorry to disappoint you,

107

Marshal. I don't know him at all, but it's not my husband.'

'Friend of mine,' grumbled Will, eyeing her thoughtfully. She had to be just about the most handsome woman he had ever seen. 'Tell me just one thing, Mrs. Denton. Why Ox-Yoke?'

She smiled with her lips but not her eyes. 'I'm sorry. Marshal, won't you please believe me when I tell you that I'm not going to help you?'

'Lady, you're not half as sorry as I am, because now I've got to lock you up as well as the colonel, and that will probably mean bad trouble. Colonel Hardin only hires tophands and good men. That means they'll be loyal to him. There's nothing wrong with that at all— except that if someone gets killed because of their loyalty, it'll be your fault.'

'No,' she murmured softly. 'It won't be my fault, Marshal, it will be your fault. You don't have to lock up Colonel Hardin. What has he done?'

'Harboured a fugitive. How does that suit you?'

'Not very well,' she said, still as cool as a snowbank. 'Because I'm not a fugitive.'

'But your husband is,' stated Will Chance.

She did not deny it. 'Marshal; it's not my husband you've found in here today, it is I, and as unhappy as this may make you, I'm not a fugitive. I'm not wanted by the law anywhere.

108

Now—where is this fugitive the colonel harboured?'

Reg Morgan walked his horse down into the yard and Dan Cowper spoke out to him from the cookshack. Will saw this and heard the exchange of words as Reg headed for the barn tie-rack upon the opposite side of the yard where he tied up, then leisurely strolled back across to the cookshack with only one glance in the direction of the main-house.

Will turned back. 'Withholding information is a misdemeanour, Mrs. Denton . . . Listen to me: I'm not out to cause you or the colonel trouble, but I want the man who robbed that coach in my territory, and if I can find him I'll get him—if I can. He's not here and maybe you're telling the truth about him never having been here, but you'll know where he is. I'll ask you just once.'

She continued to regard him coolly. It was difficult not to admire her kind of calm, quiet courage. 'Don't bother, asking,' she replied, 'because I'm not going to tell you . . . You're a stubborn man, Marshal. I've been trying to convince you for a half hour that I won't help you one bit. All I'll say is that my husband is not here.'

'Will you tell me whether or not it was you who rode that big black horse to Ox-Yoke?'

She smiled at him. 'I rode him in here, yes. Now that's the last thing I'll say to . . .'

'Mrs. Denton, you just helped me put

Colonel Hardin in jail. He told me he owned that horse; that it was an Ox-Yoke critter.' Will gestured for her to stand up, which she did, looking as steadily and unflinchingly at him as before. She was lithe and high-breasted and beautifully proportioned. She had to be about five feet and six inches which was tall for a woman.

He frankly said, 'This is a hell of a thing. You're the last person in the world I want to lock up.' He pointed. 'Out into the parlour then on out to the porch and down into the yard.'

He herded her along to the front yard over by the cookshack where he whistled and all three of his possemen came forth, shoving the cook and Colonel Hardin ahead of them.

At sight of the beautiful taffy-haired woman Cowper, Herlihy and dour Reg Morgan were mute and motionless. Colonel Hardin raised his eyes from the girl to Will Chance asking a mute question. The cook was just as dumbfounded at sight of the beautiful woman as the possemen were. At least he looked equally as dumbfounded and there was no reason to think he might be that good an actor. Finally, he too raised his eyes.

Will spoke to his townsmen when he said, 'Her name is Mrs. Denton.'

Herlihy caught the inference at once. 'Mrs. *Ladd* Denton?'

Will nodded.

Herlihy tensed, swinging his head in the direction of the main-house. 'Where is her husband?'

Will crookedly smiled. 'That's a good question. He don't seem to be around here and she refuses to say.'

Colonel Hardin raised an unsteady hand to the inside of his coat, drew forth a thin cigar and proceeded to bite off the tip, mouth the thing and then to light it. Throughout this entire ceremony his hard eyes swung from the girl to Will Chance and back again.

Through fragrant smoke he said, 'Ladd Denton is not here and he has not been here.'

Will waited in silence for whatever came next. It was a moderately long wait. The others also waited, evidently struck by the fact that their parts in what was now to ensue could not go beyond looking and listening.

'Will; this girl didn't rob that stage.'

Will had not thought she had. Even the possibility hadn't crossed his mind, although it might have later on. But there was a riddle nonetheless, so he said, 'Colonel; that black horse in the barn—the one you said belonged to you—was at the site where the stage was robbed. It was ridden by the man who stopped that stage. We tracked it . . . When you told us you followed those tracks over into town, we ran that down too . . . That horse never got any closer than about three-quarters of a mile to town, then it turned back, and that happened at night, Colonel, when no one would be likely to see the black horse or its rider. You can explain that if you'd like.'

Hardin smoked, exchanged a long look with the handsome woman, then removed his cigar and shook his head. 'I've said all I'm going to say,' he exclaimed.

Will had anticipated this so he jerked his head at Reg and Dan Herlihy. 'Saddle them both horses from the barn, and we'll head on back to town.'

As Reg and Dan departed for the barn, the girl turned a little to cast a searching glance out over the rangeland northward. It was empty as far as a person could see. The apothecary understood her look and said, 'There's not going to be anyone ride up at the last minute and save you, ma'am. That feller who rode in a while ago said the Ox-Yoke riding crew is at least four miles north-easterly cleaning waterholes.'

It was Wright Graham who finally said, 'Gawd-dammit! Will, if you do this you're going to have Waite and all our hired hands to reckon with . . . I'm warning you.'

Cowper looked a little sardonically at the cook and said nothing. Neither did Will even though the cook kept glaring as though he expected, if not a good argument, then at least *something*. Will ignored him to look at the handsome woman's profile. She was flawless.

It did not enter his mind to wonder about

her, personally, but he could not avoid wondering why anyone as strong-willed and handsome and even-dispositioned as she obviously was, would marry an outlaw and, having made *that* mistake to then also protect him.

Loyalty was a wonderful virtue—sometimes.

Will began manufacturing a cigarette. He was midway through when George Hardin said to him, 'I'd like a few words with you,' but Will finished the cigarette and lit it before eventually answering.

'We'll have plenty of time to talk in town, Colonel.'

Reg and Herlihy came forth leading the pair of saddled animals. Whatever they had discussed over yonder in the shadowy privacy of the horse-barn was known only to them, but if one were to guess from watching, one would have assumed they had discussed the outlaw's wife because neither of them took their eyes off her until everyone who could ride was mounted, then they all struck out, mostly on foot, in the direction of the creek where the tethered horses were still dozing.

Wright Graham, left behind, was rushing across to the bunkhouse and pulling off his apron as he trotted before the town-bound party got half-way to the creek. By the time Will and his possemen got their horses, led them on out into the open and mounted them to lead off for town with the prisoners, the cook had rigged out a pudding-footed big old sorrel mare and was trying to urge her over into almost any gait but her kidney-bruising trot, as he hastened forth onto the range in search of the rangeboss and the riders.

The sun was high and the clarity was gone by this time. There was a haze over everything. In a couple of months it would be full summer. Then that heat-haze would lie in layers which would heavily undulate when a rider passed through them.

Now, the haze was there but the heatwaves would not be along for a while yet. Will and his possemen had Morganton in sight on ahead by the time Wright Graham had even begun to cross Ox-Yoke's north-easterly range, and by the time they rode down into town afternoon shadows had pretty well obscured all the greater distances. Even in town, where people were beginning to think in terms of supper, there were shadows along both sides of the empty roadway.

CHAPTER THIRTEEN

THE ECHO OF TRUMPETS

People undoubtedly saw Will return with his possemen plus the two riders from Ox-Yoke, but it would still be a while before it would be generally realised that the handsome woman accompanying Constable Chance and Colonel Hardin was not just a companion.

About the time folks began to take their evening strolls—the ones who had their wives on hands—and also at about the time the men who could slip away without their wives, assembled at Herlihy's bar, the actual story of what had occurred out at Ox-Yoke would unfold, and *then* there would be plenty of comment.

Everyone knew Colonel Hardin was a bad man to cross even though he had looked mild enough as he had ridden down through town beside Constable Chance.

But the conjecture, as always in cases of this kind, trailed well behind the facts. In this instance Will had dismissed his possemen, who were delighted for an opportunity to return to their businesses, and had locked the roadside door of the jailhouse with he and his prisoners inside, before there was even an inkling that something had happened which when known would titillate the town—which would in fact titillate all of Morgan Valley.

Will did not make much of an effort to interrogate his prisoners and he made no effort at all to placate them. He took George Hardin to a cell and locked him in, then returned to the front office and stood at his desk regarding the handsome woman seated opposite him. For a long while they simply

115

regarded one another, and in this long interval Will decided that she really was not going to co-operate. He was right. After their staring-match she said, 'Marshal, you don't truly expect me to help you.'

He sat down. 'No, but it would be nice if you'd help the man who has done this much for you—he's got himself into a position even a wealthy cowman can't get out of . . . Do you owe the colonel anything?'

'Yes,' she replied candidly. 'More than you know. But he was the one who told me to consider only what I was sure had to be the best thing to do.'

'Best for who, ma'am—Colonel Hardin?'

She smiled a little. ' Just the best.'

Will studied her over a period of silence before saying, 'All right. But before I lock you up I want to tell you something. To me, your kind of loyalty is as warped as a wagon-bow. Hardin is an honest man; tough maybe and pig-headed sometimes, but honest. What he's doing now is sacrificing himself—and you're helping him do it for no better reason than to shield a man who is wanted by the law just about everywhere he has been . . . Mrs. Denton, George Hardin is worth fifty like Ladd Denton, and if you think tossing old Hardin to the wolves to save someone like Ladd Denton . . .' Will arose. 'Come along.'

As she stood, her eyes left his face briefly, ran along the far wall past the wood-stove and past the rifle-rack on the far wall, and back. There was a fleeting shadow of uncertainty and distinct pain in her lovely eyes but only for a moment, then she stoically allowed herself to be led away.

Will put her in the uppermost cell of his back cell-room. Like most jailhouses in cow-country there was no provision for female prisoners because there were rarely ever any female law-breakers.

As he closed the door and turned to lock it she said, 'If things were different I'd help.'

Will was too annoyed at her stubbornness to assess this comment properly. All he did was raise a sulphurous look and say, 'Yeah,' as he turned away heading on down to open the colonel's cell to herd him back up front into the office.

He even ordered the colonel to sit in the same chair, then he went behind his desk again and sat down, flinging the copper ring with his keys on it, atop the desk as he sighed and leaned back.

'You hungry?' he asked.

Hardin shook his head. Then he said, 'What did Antonia tell you?'

Will dwelt a moment on the name. He had not heard her given name before. 'I reckon it went the other way round, Colonel, it's more what *I* told *her.* Anyway she didn't help me any, if that's what you want to know.'

Hardin did not seem especially pleased nor

117

displeased.

'She's as stubborn as a piney-woods bull,' said Will Chance. 'I might just as well have tried to reason with a stone wall.'

'Why should she help you crucify her husband?' demanded the cowman.

'You picked a lousy word, Colonel. I'm not trying to crucify anyone and you know it. You know me that well. All I want is a stage-robber, and I'm going to get him!'

Hardin said, 'And you called *her* stubborn!'

Will's retort was curt. 'It's not the same and you darned well know it, Colonel . . . Leave her out of it for a minute or two. Why did you lie to me about that black horse; why have you hidden her even from your own riders; why did you neglect to tell me an outlaw's woman was in Morgan Valley?'

Hardin loosened in the chair looking more tired than deeply troubled, and that was probably in character; he was a man who had lived with fierce and thunderous carnage, as well as all the terrible disasters which had followed in its wake. This kind of dilemma he was now in despite its menace to his reputation and local standing, probably could not compare with most of the wartime scenes he had been a part of, and actually, as he proved when next he spoke, his current involvement entailed something which to most men was basically quite simple.

'Will, when you're my age you'll have doubts

118

about a lot of things which now, at your age, seem clearly definable as black and white.'

The younger man hid a yawn and said, 'I'm listening, Colonel.'

'I've seen nations born and I've seen them die,' Hardin averred. 'I've seen thousands of men who knew absolutely they were in the right, get overrun by men who weren't fighting for a nation as much as they were fighting and dying for principles. Will . . . I can tell you this: when it comes right down to it, your strengths and your loyalties belong to your own kind. Almost everything else will change until you can't recognise it over the years, but your own flesh and blood are a part of you; you belong as much to them as they belong to you, and *that* is permanent.'

Will slowly frowned, a glimmer beginning to form in his mind.

Colonel Hardin jerked his head to indicate the closed cell-room door across the room behind him. 'That is my daughter in there.'

Will's breath stopped short in his chest. After a stunned moment had passed he leaned, picked up that yellow telegraph form and handed it wordlessly to the older man. The telegram related in statistical crispness that George Hardin, late colonel of the Confederate Army, had married one Amanda Currier before the war and they'd had a son listed as George Hardin's dependant when Hardin had been parolled at the conclusion of hostilities.

Hardin read the message, tossed it back and raised quizzical eyes to Will's face. He was just now beginning to grasp something. '. . . You thought her husband was my son?' Hardin asked.

Will pointed. 'The War Department didn't mention a daughter, Colonel, just a son.'

'Will, that telegram was compiled from the parole records made at the end of the war. My daughter was born six years *after* the war. Her mother died then, at the birthing. I quit the South, left Antonia with my sister in Virginia to come out here where I didn't know a soul and didn't see a single thing to remind me of anything back there . . . Anything at all.' Hardin paused to faintly frown again at Will. 'You thought Ladd Denton was my son?'

Will shrugged almost defensively. 'All I had to go on was a lie you told me about her black horse, Colonel, and that telegram.' Will leaned both elbows atop the desk. 'Colonel; why in hell did you tell her to sacrifice you in order to save *him?*'

'Because she is young and so is her husband, and maybe he'll change, but you see I've just about run my course . . . Will, I just tried to explain something to you about where a person's loyalties lie.'

'Yeah, I heard you, Colonel, but by gawd this time you're as wrong as she is. Ladd Denton is bad clear through . . . Wait a minute,

Colonel, let me finish. Denton's as old as I am and he's still doing things even wild young cowboys know better than to do . . .' Will paused and steadily stared at the older man as an errant realisation came to him. The colonel's *real* trouble was that now, in his sundown years, he saw something he had learned to cherish—his kinship with his remaining family—also turning bad before his eyes, and he could not or would not allow himself to look. This was all he had left.

Will said, 'Care for a cup of coffee?'

Hardin shook his head. 'No thanks. Maybe you'd better lock me back into the cell, I'm tired.'

Will nodded. 'One more question, Colonel.'

Hardin got a sardonic expression on his face as he leaned to arise. 'Will, I'm not going to tell you where he is. Anyway, he's probably not still there.' The colonel arose and waited for the lawman to do the same, then as they crossed the room old Hardin sounded weary when he said, 'She's the spitting image of her mother.'

Will looked up. 'Her mother must have been a beautiful woman.'

As Hardin passed through the doorway he agreed with that assessment. 'She was. And she was just as good as she was handsome.'

They passed the girl's cell. Hardin looked in and smiled but Will refused to turn his head, but after he had locked her father in and had turned down the overhead lantern so that the older man could rest if he chose to, Will went back up there, unlocked her cell and jerked his head for her to precede him into the office.

He was more angry than indignant.

Antonia Denton went almost stolidly to the chair she had vacated earlier, and sat. Will went to the wood-stove to pitch in paper and kindling, then to place his granite-ware jailhouse coffee pot atop the stove. When he turned towards the desk she said, 'Marshal, it's been a very tiring day.'

He looked down unsympathetically. 'Yeah; but not as tiring for you as for your father.'

She turned and looked out one of the high little barred roadside windows where full darkness lurked the full length of Morganton's main thoroughfare. 'Well—so you know,' she murmured, and looked back at him.

His retort was curt. 'No, I don't know. Like I said before, you're sacrificing a good man for a bad one.' He sank down at the desk. 'I don't understand you. I don't understand how you can do something like this . . . I don't see how in hell the colonel could produce something like you.'

She did not reproach him for this condemnation. All she said was, 'May I go back to my cell?'

'Yes. After you answer one question for me.'

'Marshal, I'm still not going to help you track down my husband.'

'The hell with your husband, lady. Just tell me what possible comparison you can make between Ladd Denton and George Hardin?'

She caught her underlip between her teeth and held it as she looked steadily at Will, then she said, 'Marshal, as long as you know some of it, I'll tell you a little more of it. My father did not raise me, his sister did back in Virginia. I did not even see my father until four years ago when my husband found him out here, and I rode to Ox-Yoke to tell him who I was . . . Marshal; to whom do I owe loyalty, the father I never knew or the man I loved?'

Will was too inherently honest to make the easy judgement. He wanted to, because he was a lawman and her husband was an outlaw, but he did not make it. He arose and crossed to the cell-room and opened the door for her without speaking.

When he was locking her back into the cell she leaned to softly make a revelation. 'Even though he sent me back here. Even though he came as far as the rocks up there where he robbed that stage, and even though he told me the last time I saw him that he did not want to be burdened with a wife any more. I still can't do it, Marshal. I still can't betray him.'

Will went back to the desk, barred the cell-room door, flung down the keys and stood a moment listening to the coffee boil. Then he removed the pot, set it aside to cool, did not draw off a cup after all, and locked up his jailhouse for the night.

On the stroll up in the direction of the boarding-house he watched the livid brilliance of a shooting star make a gash across the underbelly of heaven.

The echoes of a war whose reverberations were still coming back more than a quarter century later, had just touched his life too, back there at the jailhouse.

CHAPTER FOURTEEN

BETWEEN A ROCK AND A HARD PLACE

In the morning when Will Chance appeared at the cafe for an early breakfast and two trays, the hulking old rangerider who operated the place leaned down in front of the lawman without smiling, his craggy face tough-set and his steely old eyes like cooling lava.

'You're pickin' on one of the best rangemen in Morgan Valley,' he announced. 'I rode for Colonel Hardin about the time you was born, Constable. He was a good man then and he's still a good man.'

Will's first reaction was to order breakfast and overlook the cafeman's smouldering hostility. His second reaction was different. 'When you worked for Hardin,' he asked, ' did he ever mention children? I mean, did he ever mention having children?'

The truculent cafeman blinked. He had expected almost any kind of reaction to his hostility but this reaction. 'What the hell are you talking about—children?'

'Did he mention a son or a daughter?'

'Colonel Hardin?'

Will scowled. 'We weren't talking about Santa Claus were we? Yes, damn it, Colonel Hardin.'

'No, he never mentioned children. In fact he never talked of his wife but once, and that was Christmas time when we all pitched in to drag down a tree from the mountains and string popcorn to decorate it with. He said something Christmas night when we was all over at the main-house drinking his brandy. He said he'd give ten years off his life if his wife could have been there. That's the only time I ever knew him to talk about her, and I rode for him off and on, seasonally, for seven years. And by gawd there was never a fairer man to work for.'

Will settled at the counter. 'Coffee,' he ordered, 'fried spuds, breakfast steak and toast.'

The cafeman was not ready to retreat behind his kitchen curtain. 'I don't see nothin' wrong with him protectin' Denton's wife, Constable, and maybe if there was more chivalry round nowadays it'd be a better world.'

'Maybe,' conceded Will. 'Why don't you just rassle up my breakfast and let me worry about the colonel?'

'Because I heard at the saloon last night you might be fixing to take it out on the colonel because you can't catch that lousy stage-robber. And Constable, I don't need no customer in here who—'

'Wait a minute,' snapped Will. 'That is a lousy lie.'

'You haven't caught him yet have you?' growled the larger older man.

'No, and I haven't knocked you on your butt either, but that is going to happen very soon now—too.' Will pointed in the direction of the curtained-off cooking area. 'Just get the food will you, damn it all. As for that highwayman— I know who he is and when I get a chance I'll nail him. Does that suit you or do you want this damned badge and the job that goes with it? No? Then get my damned breakfast!'

The cafeman was red in the face. Perhaps twenty or thirty years earlier he and Will Chance would have locked horns right there across the counter, except that thirty years earlier the cafeman had been big and powerful and in his prime and Will Chance had been a yearling. A *long* yearling.

Later, when the two fuming individuals were out of each other's sight and the cafe was fragrantly steamy in the pre-sunrise early morning, Doctor Spence came ambling in looking as though he had been swilling Cowper's home-brew most of last night when in fact he had been four miles out on the north-easterly range delivering a baby to a cowman's wife which he'd had to take by belly-section, something that drained the spirit as well as the energy from a man as conscientious as Doc Spence was.

He sat down near Will, nodded his head and did not say a word, which was perhaps just as well.

Five minutes later when the cafeman came forth with the lawman's breakfast on a large old crockery platter Doc Spence looked over, then ordered the same thing, asking that the coffee be brought first, and as the embittered cafeman glared then stalked off, Doc looked around in mild surprise.

'What the devil bit him this morning?' he asked of Will, and got a curt answer.

'I did.'

Spence's weariness seemed to slowly drop away as he sat and silently studied Will with the identical expression of surprise he had used in his examination of the cafeman's surly countenance. Afterwards he made a rattling loud sigh and hunched forward awaiting his coffee in total silence.

Not until Will had finished eating and was balancing the two trays as he headed for the door did Doctor Spence look up again, and that was only to step back, open the door for

Will and afterwards close it behind him as the cafeman peered from behind his curtain to glare doorward and make an uncomplimentary comment.

'Danged whippersnapper went and locked up Colonel Hardin and his daughter last night.'

Spence raised round eyes. 'Locked up . . . whose daughter?'

'You heard right, Doc. George Hardin's daughter.'

'He doesn't have . . .'

'Oh yes he does, Doc. If you doubt me go and ask Dan Herlihy. Him and Reg and Dan Cowper was out at Ox-Yoke yesterday. They went out looking for someone else and they brang back the colonel and his daughter. Will's got them locked up across the road. Damnedest injustice I ever heard of.'

Hubert Spence arose, dropped silver beside his plate and walked out of the cafe into a soft dawn-lighted morning which was as delicate and soft-coloured as most springtime mornings were in the mid-range country.

Morganton was coming to life again. Abe Neve had his general store open and Abe plus his clerk were putting out their sidewalk display—over which the Town Council was locked in stubborn dispute since one of them tripped over a ten-gallon milk can and tore the knees out of his britches, and now wanted an ordinance to ban all sidewalk displays.

Doctor Spence watched Abe and his clerk for a moment, then turned to study the facade of the jail-house upon the opposite side of the wide roadway. He started over there, but at the last moment hesitated when Henry Devereaux hailed him from the corral-yard gate and beckoned with an upflung arm.

He sang out up the street. 'What is it, Henry?'

'I got one with Monday-morning complaint, Doc,' Devereaux sang back.

Doc looked disgusted. 'Darn it, Henry, you know what to do for aztoria, you don't need me. And if you were a better horseman you wouldn't have something like that anyway.'

Devereaux reddened. This entire short exchange had been audible up as far as Herlihy's saloon. Henry turned with a ripped-out curse and stamped back into his corral-yard and Doctor Spence continued on to the door-way of the jailhouse where he vigorously knocked.

Will opened up and scowled. 'No one in here is sick, Doc.'

Spence pushed past with a sarcastic comment. 'I didn't know you had studied medicine, Will.' He stopped and turned from side to side. 'Where are they —George Hardin and the girl?'

Will pointed to his cell-room door. 'Down there. And what of it?'

'May I see George?'

'What for, Doc?'

Spence went to a chair and leaned with both hands upon the back of it. 'Will, what are you so disagreeable about this morning? George Hardin and I've been friends for thirty years. Is that enough reason for one man to want to see another man—who is in trouble? . . . Is it true that he had a daughter?'

'Thirty years,' muttered Will, picking up the keyring. 'You and the colonel were bosom-friends for thirty years and you have to ask me if he had a daughter. Come along, Doc, and don't keep him from eating his breakfast. I just took down their trays.'

As the two men marched past Antonia's cell Doctor Spence turned with candid interest and stared, then he went along to the lower end of the room.

Will turned back and stopped when the handsome woman said, 'Who is that man?'

'Local physician,' explained Will. 'He and your paw been friends a long time . . . Antonia?'

'Yes?'

'Where is your brother?'

She turned violet eyes on him. 'Dead, Marshal. He died during a typhoid epidemic right after the war, down in Alexandria.' She moved closer to the bars. 'You really care about what happens to the colonel don't you?'

'I care about what happens to anyone,' he corrected her. 'That's why I'm a lousy lawman

. . . And I figured it had to be something like that—about your brother—because last night the colonel just sort of eased the conversation plumb around and got me side-tracked away from the subject.'

'Marshal; knowing him, can you imagine what it must have been like back in those days? He lost a country, all his heroes, most of his splendid ideals—and his only son, all within a space of a few years. And later, he also lost the only woman he evidently ever genuinely loved.'

Will considered her, and shook his head. She was a contrast to him. She was going to sacrifice her father for an outlaw who apparently no longer wanted her, and at the same time she understood her father perhaps better than anyone else understood him, and could feel all the anguish her father had once felt.

'I can imagine something else,' he told her. 'What it must be like seeing the only kin you got left, using you to save someone not fit to stand in your shadow.'

He left her looking after him, returned to the office and went over by a roadside window to roll and light his after-breakfast cigarette.

When Doctor Spence came up out of there a little later, looking grave, Will said, 'Close the door, Doc.'

Spence obeyed, walked over near the desk and looked up at Will. 'I haven't seen too

131

many people age overnight, have you, Will?' he asked, and did not await an answer. 'What are you holding him for? Trying to protect the only family he still has? Will; how often have you heard how hard and uncompromising he is? Go down there this morning and look at him. He's not the same George Hardin he was, only yesterday.'

Will blew smoke while continuing to gaze out into the cool, sunbright roadway where a thin trickle of early morning traffic was beginning to stir dust.

All this was happening, he told himself, over a six-hundred-dollar-robbery up the stage road a few miles. An old man he had known a few years back, who had once been a lawman down along the Texas-Mexican line, had once told him that when a lawman uncovers a crime all he really does is uncover the *surface* of something which can and usually does touch at least a dozen and sometimes two dozen lives.

He turned. 'Doc; I'm just the constable. I didn't cause any of this mess. I'm just the feller they pay to apprehend felons and whatnot— and to also haul kids down out of apple trees and to go catch horses and even milk cows folks swear up and down have been stolen and which have really only busted loose from their picket pins . . . What am I holding him for?'

'Yes.'

'I suppose for being loyal to his daughter . . . I'm going to turn him out directly.'

Doctor Spence nodded. 'What about her?'

'Go talk to her, Doc, then come back and tell me how heroic she is.'

'No thanks. If she belongs to Ladd Denton that'll be quite enough for me . . . It's been a long time since I've felt sorry for anyone as old as George Hardin is, Will.' Doctor Spence moved tiredly to the door. 'But I certainly do feel sorry for him.'

Will waited until the older man had the door opened, before saying. 'I feel sorry for him too, Doc. I even feel sorry for her—and for you—and what does that have to do with me doing my job?'

Spence did not answer. He closed the door gently after himself and went tiredly off in the direction of his cottage.

Will continued to lean and look out the window and smoke his after-breakfast cigarette.

CHAPTER FIFTEEN

NEWS!

Will brought Colonel Hardin to the office and offered him coffee, which the older man accepted, and sat across the desk as he sipped java.

He did not look any older to Will, nor had

Will really expected him to look older; Doctor Spence had been speaking metaphorically, of course, and in this regard Will was willing to concede there was a difference between the uncompromising, rich and powerful cowman Hardin had always been up until now, and the way he sat there now drinking black coffee and looking somehow detached, or at least looking remote from things.

Will said, 'Colonel, if he sent her home why don't you accept it that he don't want her?'

Hardin spoke without raising his eyes. 'Will, you've never been married. All married folks have arguments, and it's not uncommon for someone to head for home—sent there or voluntarily going there.'

Will did not dispute this but he had another aspect of the same problem. 'If she was my daughter and someone like Ladd Denton turned her loose I'd keep her home away from him, and I'd be tickled pink they were apart.'

This time the older man raised his head. 'You don't know what you'd do,' he said with a little of the old-time Hardin spirit. 'You've never been in this position . . . You are completely ignorant of affairs like these, Will. Completely.' Hardin finished the coffee and ran a hand up his bristly cheek. 'Do you have a razor I could borrow?'

Will had one. In fact he had several razors in the desk, left behind over the years by hastily departing jail inmates, but instead of

134

offering a razor he said, 'Colonel, you can go down to the liverybarn, saddle up and head for home. You're free to go.'

Hardin stared. 'Since when do you make the laws?' he asked, his testiness increasing momentarily, the other slumped and taciturn, demoralised old man becoming less and less evident. 'You arrested me for harbouring a criminal, and that still stands, don't it?'

Will looked a little pained. 'No, it don't still stand. Just shag your butt out of here. You're free. Why don't you just accept that and go?'

'Because my daughter is here, and as long as she stays so do I.'

'The hell you do,' exclaimed Will, then checked his rising annoyance. 'Colonel; the girl stays for a little while longer. Maybe I can turn her out too, later on.'

'She'll never tell you where her husband is,' stated George Hardin. 'Never.'

An idea flashed through Will's consciousness, coming out of nowhere. 'She don't have to tell me.'

Hardin's brows dropped a notch. 'You know?'

'Nothing like the telegraph,' murmured Will.

Instantly Hardin came to the outlaw's defence. 'He won't still be over there. Men of his kind keep moving, always.'

'All right, but he can't come over this way, and if he goes down south where they know him he's going to ride right into trouble. What does that leave?'

Colonel Hardin made a wide arm-gesture. 'The way is open all the way to Canada,' he averred, and Will slowly shook his head.

'They're setting up man-hunting posses all along his route . . . Colonel; you're as bad as the girl; you're trying to defend that worthless bastard too. And why? After he abandoned her?'

'I told you, Will. They just had a little tiff. It happens all the time between married folks.'

'Colonel, tell me something. Did you want her to marry Ladd Denton?'

'That's a poor question,' stated the older man. 'She was married to him before I knew she wasn't still back in Virginia. The first time she arrived at Ox-Yoke and introduced herself, she was married to him.'

'Colonel, if you had known she was fixing to marry Ladd Denton, and could have done anything about it, would you have tried to stop the marriage?'

'Yes, But none of those things happened, Will. Like I just told you she was—'

'Colonel, damn it all, now is your chance. He sent her back. She knows he sent her back. This might be the best chance you'll ever have to really do something for her.'

What George Hardin's reaction to this might have been, he got no prompt opportunity to manifest it. Charley Graham walked in from the roadway, looked owlishly at the cowman, handed over a sealed slip of mustard-coloured paper and without a single word to anyone turned and marched back out again.

Will had a chance to partially open the telegram, then there was a second early-morning interruption. This time the unsmiling man who walked in was armed and dusty and bronzed from days in the saddle. It was Waite Culpepper from Ox-Yoke.

Will had been expecting him. In fact Will had been expecting the entire Ox-Yoke riding crew, so he nodded without smiling at the rangeboss, then stepped to a front wall window and looked out.

They were there, armed with Winchesters as well as sixguns, loafing at the tie-rack out front looking willing to take on the entire town if they had to. Will stepped back towards the desk just as Colonel Hardin said, 'Thanks for coming,' to Waite, and the rangeboss soberly nodded towards his employer without once taking his eyes off the lawman.

'We'll take him back with us,' Waite said quietly, making no move towards the gun he wore but clearly ready to make such a move.

Will was sardonic. 'Colonel, I told you to go fifteen minutes ago. Now I guess you'd better do it.'

Hardin with armed reinforcements was the same man he had been before, without them.

'I don't leave this place until my daughter goes with me.'

That statement brought Culpepper's head around. He stared but said nothing.

Will did not yield. 'When I've had another talk with her,' he said. 'Until then she stays—and you go.'

Waite was still staring at Hardin when Will turned towards him. 'You can have him, Culpepper. Get him out of here.'

The rangeboss turned back towards Will, hostility showing but not markedly showing. Waite Culpepper's loyalty to his employer was reasonable enough; it was no more than was expected of him, but on the other hand he and Will Chance had been friends a long time. Eventually the rangeboss asked a question.

'If you don't want to hold him, Will, why in hell did you arrest him and fetch him down here to the jailhouse?'

The answer to that lay with Colonel Hardin. Will's reply was to that effect. 'On the ride back to Ox-Yoke you ask him,' answered Will, acting as though Colonel Hardin were not there. 'I thought he was guilty of something that evidently he wasn't guilty of. It was a reasonable mistake.'

Waite turned. 'You ready, Colonel?'

Hardin, the man Doctor Spence had felt so sorry for because Spence had seen him as a demoralised, pathetic old man, glared. 'No, I'm not ready.'

138

'But Will said you can go.'

'Yes, and you darn well heard what I told him about that, didn't you? I don't budge out of here until my daughter is released.'

This time the rangeboss put into words what he had only signified understanding of before by staring. 'I didn't know you had a daughter, Colonel.'

Will started to speak when Charley Graham poked his head in the doorway from the roadway and said, 'Well, confound it, aren't you ever goin' to send an answer!'

Will was still holding that folded telegram. Until this minute he had forgotten all about it. He stepped closer to the front-wall-window and unfolded the paper to read its message.

In terse words the telegram said there had been a stage coach robbery north of Livermore, which was the next town northward of Morganton, the previous evening, and it was thought the outlaws were heading southward, which would be in the direction of Morgan Valley.

Will slowly cast a sidelong look at George Hardin, then he faced the telegrapher and said, 'No, I'm not going to send a message, Charley. There is nothing to say—if they're heading south we'll do what we can.' Graham looked at George Hardin, at Waite Culpepper, back to the town marshal again, then with a look of enormous disgust he pulled back and slammed the door.

Will stepped behind his desk, folded the yellow slip of paper slowly and pocketed it. He said, 'Colonel, get your butt out of here or I'm going to throw it out.'

Hardin was a perceptive individual. He had listened to all that exchange between the constable and the telegrapher. Now he said, 'Who's heading south, Will?'

The telegram had not identified the outlaws. Even if it had Will probably would not have named them for Hardin. 'You've got a minute,' said Will. 'Waite; you better get him moving.'

Culpepper looked at his employer, worried and baffled, but he said nothing. Not even when Will started around the desk.

Hardin arose quickly from his chair. He had correctly read the expression on Constable Chance's face as the lawman came around the desk after him.

'I'll be outside,' he said, reddening. 'And I'll stay out there until you release her. Do you understand?'

Will did not reply. There was nothing to reply about. He had agreed to release her— after he'd had another talk with her. Will gestured for Waite to open the door, then he herded them both outside, dropped the *tranca* into place which barred the door from inside, and still feeling yeasty enough to argue, he went over to the cell-room door and yanked it back.

Antonia Denton was waiting when Will released her, and walked behind her to the office and pointed to a chair. The same chair her father had recently occupied. 'I know where he is,' Will said, looking down at the beautiful woman.

She did not even scoff. 'All right, Marshal. It was going to happen, wasn't it? But I wasn't going to be the one to—'

'Cut that out,' he growled at her. 'Your loyalty makes me sick to my stomach . . . He robbed another coach last night. Up by Livermore.'

'What do you want me to do about it?' she asked.

'Tell me who is riding with him.'

She sat and gazed at Will for a long while. Then shook her head. 'I meant it. I wouldn't help you one bit. I won't tell you a thing, Marshal.'

'Then,' said Will, 'I'll kill him and you can have that to carry around with you the rest of your life.'

'How?' she demanded.

'He is heading south from Livermore. I've got the telegraph message about that, and I've got several darned good men who'll help me set up the ambush.'

Antonia stared upwards as though she were trying her utmost to determine either Will's chances of success, or perhaps she was trying to make up her mind whether he was speaking the truth or not.

Finally, she said, 'What do you want me to do?'

He looked stonily back. 'Not a damned thing. Nothing. I'm going to settle up for you—and for the colonel. You didn't have the decency or the guts to do it for your father and for your own darned self-respect, so I'll do it for you.'

She said, 'Just a minute, Constable.' Then she sat a while longer looking at him, and finally she arose to walk to a window and look out where the golden sunshine was.

She saw her father and his crew out there, saw the peaceful little town, saw riders making their leisurely way into and out of town. She turned back to face Will.

'I doubt that you'll be able to do it, Constable, because Ladd is a very deadly gunman . . . And he'll have three men with him who are almost as good with guns. Their names are Chuck Torrey, Al Garmon and Pete Lester.'

'Wanted men?'

She nodded. 'Wanted in Texas, New Mexico Territory and Colorado.' She returned from the window to the chair. 'Marshal, let me go out there with you.'

He stared at her. 'What in hell for? That won't be a picnic.'

'Just let me—'

'Lady, you go back in your cell.' Will

gestured for her to move back towards the cell-room.

She arose immediately and obeyed. Even when he was locking her in, she did not offer to argue, but her gaze did not leave his face until he turned in the doorway and said, 'Maybe I don't blame Denton for shedding you.' He did not explain what he meant by that, he simply closed the door.

She held to the front strap-steel bars of the cell waiting rigidly to hear him lock the cell-room door from the far side.

He did not lock it.

CHAPTER SIXTEEN

AMBUSH!

When Will left the jailhouse he locked the front door from the outside, a precaution he would have naturally taken in any event since he had a prisoner locked in one of the cells, but the Ox-Yoke men were still out there, loafing at his tie rack, so he took a double precaution.

Neither Colonel Hardin nor Waite Culpepper were there but all the other riders were, and they gravely watched as the jailhouse door was locked, then one of them said, 'Hey, Marshal, you figure us four is going

143

to clean out the office?'

Will turned, singled out the speaker—Lon Stearn, the man Will had locked up overnight—and said, 'No, I wasn't fearful you'd raid the place, Lon. But I've got some rotgut in there and in your case the temptation might be overwhelming.'

No one laughed. No one was supposed to laugh. Will hung there a moment but none of the other riders were going to take it up, and Lon got red in the face and looked for a moment as though he might take exception, but he didn't.

Will walked down to the shoeing-shed and told Reg they had to ride out. Reg was drinking from an old mud *olla*. There was sweat dripping from him. It was hot work, shoeing team-horses, just about any time, but on a hot day inside a building with a corrugated-iron roof, it was deadly. Reg turned, spat water, turned back and nodded at Will.

As Will turned back in the direction of the roadway he heard Reg call to someone named Asa and tell Asa to finish up the team-horse.

Will went up to the apothecary shop and nearly collided with Doctor Spence who was just leaving the shop. Will curtly nodded and shouldered on past. Doc turned as though he might engage Will in conversation, but Will kept right on going until he was across the room, then he leaned and said, 'We got to ride,

144

Dan. Reg's already rigging out.'

Cowper watched Doctor Spence shrug and walk away scowling before he said, 'Right now?'

'Right damned now!'

'This won't be another wild-goose chase will it, because I've got a half-dozen prescriptions I'd ought to be compounding today.'

Will reached and lightly tapped the older man's shoulder. 'Bring your Colt, some extra rounds, and your saddlegun with more extra rounds. We'll be at the barn in ten or fifteen minutes.'

Will was already moving briskly away when Cowper called, 'Hey, damn it, what is this all about?'

'Catching the man who robbed the coach and got some of your money,' replied Will. 'Interested?'

Cowper didn't answer but he reached back to loosen the strings holding his short little apron.

Will cut diagonally across towards Herlihy's place, and the moment he entered he saw Culpepper and Colonel Hardin. They were at a table solemnly talking. Will saw their eyes lift to him and ignored them both as he reached the bar and leaned.

'Bring your guns and some extra rounds,' he told the barman. 'We'll be leaving from the liverybarn in a few minutes.'

'Hold it, damn it,' growled the bar-owner.

'What is it?'

'The man who robbed the coach.'

Herlihy's face abruptly smoothed out. 'You got a line on him?'

'Better than that, Dan, we're going out to lay a snare for him. He's on his way back to Morgan Valley.'

'Why that son of a bitch,' said Dan Herlihy, and began moving up towards the younger man who was also working his bar, to explain why he would be unable to finish out the day.

Will headed for his shed out back of the jailhouse. He was rigging his horse when Hardin and Culpepper came around there to stand in the doorway watching him for a moment before the colonel said, 'I thought you said you were going to turn her loose.'

Will was annoyed at their intrusion right at this moment. He cinched up and leaned to adjust the two straps of his saddleboot before shoving the Winchester into the thing. 'Colonel,' he replied evenly, 'right now there is something more important to be done. When I get back we'll talk about Miz Denton.'

Waite Culpepper, thumbs hooked in his shellbelt, stood solidly in the shed opening. He did not open his mouth, he did not allow his eyes to leave Will Chance, and he made no move to get out of the way.

Hardin seemed just as adamant. 'Will; we're both going to live a long while after this is over with. What's the sense in storing up the

146

material for bad memories of it?'

The lawman gazed across leather at George Hardin, wondering if that was how old men viewed approaching trouble. He decided that it probably was, then he stepped from behind his horse—Colt in hand.

'Get out of the doorway,' he said to Waite.

Culpepper had made a common mistake; he had underestimated someone. In most instances mistakes of this kind could be forgiven. It was difficult to overlook it, though, when the man who had been underestimated turned up to be holding a pistol.

Culpepper looked from the gun to Will's face and moved away from the shed opening. Colonel Hardin also looked from the gun to the face of the man holding it, then he also left the shed, walking out front of it and standing over there near his rangeboss.

Will walked forth, turned and led his horse towards the front roadway. Not a word was said. He led the horse the full distance keeping it between himself and those two men back yonder.

In fact he led the horse all the way down to the liverybarn where Herlihy, Cowper and Morgan were waiting, having just finished rigging up.

There was strong interest at the liverybarn but none of the possemen opened their mouths. They got astride and headed up out of town in a jog. People saw them and turned to see them again. There was no way to mistake a lawman leading three other men out of a town, all of them fully armed, for anything but trouble-hunters. Morganton had as active a gossip grapevine as any other cowtown; within a very short while, now, speculation would be rife the full length and breadth of the town limits.

As far as Will Chance was concerned people could speculate all they cared to, his own thoughts, like his objectives, were elsewhere.

For example, while there were a dozen ways to reach Morgan Valley from up north, the most common way—as well as the easiest since it avoided all the surrounding mountains—was by way of the stage-road, the same road which ran north and south through the valley. The same road, in fact, which passed those northward rocks where the stage-robbery had occurred.

But Will also had to consider all the trails from the north because clearly any party of fleeing outlaws would anticipate their misdeeds preceding them and would be wary.

He knew every trail, including the unused ancient Indian trails, but as they were approaching the rocks where all this trouble had started, he detached Reg Morgan to scout westerly, and Dan Herlihy to scout easterly. His instructions were simple.

'If you see four men riding apart from the road, get back to me right away. Don't try to buck them and don't let them see you.'

Will and Dan Cowper rode on up the roadway watching their friends diverge. Cowper swung forward in the saddle to also examine the onward stage-road as far as it was visible. 'Why in hell would Denton come back here?' he asked. 'He knows folks are looking for a stage-robber. He's not so dumb he don't realise that.'

Will looked around. 'Did you know Colonel Hardin had a daughter?'

Cowper stared. 'A daughter? No.'

'Then you wouldn't know Colonel Hardin's daughter is married to Ladd Denton, would you?'

This was too much for pragmatic Dan Cowper to swallow. 'Come off it,' he growled. 'What do you take me for?'

'It just happens to be true,' stated Will, and straightened in the saddle as he swung to look far out left and right. Reg had stopped but Herlihy was still riding. Will watched Reg Morgan and when Cowper started to say something Will held up a silencing hand. Cowper fell silent, still looking very sceptical as he too swung to look out where Reg Morgan was evidently intently staring at something up-country and to his left.

Reg turned back abruptly, loping in the direction of the roadway, but he halted out a half mile and gestured with his upraised carbine. Will swung to seek the bar-owner.

149

Herlihy was still loping eastward. He was almost too far by now to see a signal if they could have caught his attention long enough to have sent one.

Cowper said, 'Let's go, it can't be helped about Dan.'

They left the road riding straight for Morgan, and before they reached him Reg used his carbine to point far overland and up-country. 'Four horsemen heading south,' he reported. 'You keep lookin' and you'll see them.'

Will stood in his stirrups and squinted, then he slowly made a survey in every other direction. The only riders in sight were those four oncoming men who were apparently willing to parallel the stage-road on their southward flight but were unwilling to get any closer to it.

Soon now the distant riders would make out three men heading in their direction. Cowper considered, then made a reasonable assessment of all this. 'If they're not Denton and his crew, then they've got to be four men travelling through. But travellers use the road. If they've got a good reason for *not* using it I can't figure out what it might be, so let's go ask them.'

'And if it's *not* travellers,' asked Reg dourly, 'What do you do when they shoot you, Dan?'

Will spoke before the apothecary could answer. 'Fan out just a little. By now they see

150

us.' As his companions widened their gap a little, the oncoming four horsemen drew down to a steady slow walk, and instead of spreading out as the possemen had done, the strangers bunched up closer. Evidently they were talking because as Will got closer he could see heads shaking or nodding.

He had an instinctive feeling that the foremost man up there was indeed the notorious and legendary outlaw Ladd Denton. Will eased off the tie-down on his Colt and leaned to loosen the Winchester. On both sides of him his possemen did the same. By the time the two parties of riders were close enough to discern the details of the men and horses in front of them it became clear that neither party was going to yield, was not going to turn and ride away from the other party.

Dan Cowper called softly to Will. 'Trouble's coming.'

He had scarcely got the words out when the oncoming mounted men arrived at their unanimous decision, apparently. They spurred their horses up a little, then sank in the hooks and charged. Will and his two friends had expected almost anything but a savage sudden attack.

One of the strangers had a carbine in his fist. He fired one-handedly, levered the weapon one-handedly by dropping it low then snapping it smartly upwards. He was clearly an experienced carbine-man.

Will heard the shot and looked at his friends. They were both pulling out booted Winchesters. Will palmed his sixgun even though the distance was still too great. He booted out his horse in a dead-ahead run straight at the charging outlaws. He did not aim except to tilt the gunbarrel when he thought they had to be about in hand-gun range, and fired.

On both sides of him Cowper and Morgan also spurred at the oncoming gunmen. Both of them fired from the shoulder, and one of them dropped a horse. The animal folded its legs and simply dropped, then rolled, catapulting its rider end over end. Where the rider stopped rolling, he lay sprawled and unmoving; injured or dead he was out of the fight and that evened the odds.

Now, they were all firing, three men charging up-country and three men charging down-country. It still had not been positively determined that these were the outlaws Will Chance wanted, but there was no way to halt the scrap now to find out.

Reg Morgan rode with his reins high-held in the same hand he was steadying his Winchester with. Cowper rode lower, as though he knew about this kind of combat. He fired just once, then swerved as someone fired back at him. He acted as though he knew exactly how to act in this affair.

Will picked out the foremost man and did

not take his eyes off him. They came straight at one another. The outlaw threw a handgun shot and missed by two hundred yards. Firing from the back of a racing horse was never accurate. Will held a closer bead and saw the outlaw wince as he fired, and was encouraged to try again.

At that exact moment his cantle rose up like a maul and slammed him in the back, the horn and swells fell away in front, and before Will fully understood what had happened, his horse was up-ending. He kicked both feet free and hurled himself sidewards. The animal struck and skidded and flopped dead before he finished tumbling.

Will had not heard the carbine-shot which had done this. All he saw was that foremost man leering as he rode in low, gun extended, to finish the kill.

CHAPTER SEVENTEEN

DEAD MEN!

For Will Chance who had faced many kinds of trouble before and after becoming a peace officer, this particular moment was the worst. It might have helped if his fall had caused senselessness, or even if it had temporarily stunned him, but although he felt slightly breathless as he scrabbled around on both hands and grabbed for the sixgun lying close by, his mind was perfectly clear.

The dead horse lay fifteen feet distant, above him to the right and left men were now firing sixguns instead of carbines, and bearing straight at him, looking fierce and exultant, sixgun shoved outward and aimed downward, rode that formidable man who had led the initial charge of the strangers.

Will could see the man aiming, could feel the man's finger tightening. He flopped frantically sideways as the horseman rode him down. He rolled as fast as possible and felt the horse's hooves lightly brush him as the charging rider, seeing that he had missed with the gun, reined the horse to ride up and over Will Chance.

Somewhere a man yelled, and Will heard but did not heed this. He did not even realise that the gunfight above and behind him was dwindling. All he knew was that the big savage-looking man who had tried so hard to ride him down was hauling his horse around, gun high and cocked, readying himself and his horse for a second run.

Will rolled over, came up onto one knee, raised his Colt one-handed, threw up a supporting forearm and took aim. When he fired the stranger had completed his turn, was squaring up to begin his charge.

The bullet struck the man high and hard.

The reaction was instantaneous; the big man was punched hard back against his cantle, his gun-hand wavered then began coming down.

Will cocked, steadied up, and squeezed off his second shot.

This time the mounted man visibly wilted. His rein-hand opened and the reins trailed, his right hand came steadily lower, dropped the cocked sixgun and made an ineffectual grab for mane-hair, missed, and the man fell like a sack of wet meal.

Will waited. The riderless horse plunged past but his rider did not move. For ten seconds Will waited. Someone far back called fiercely. 'Drop it you son of a bitch!'

Will became aware that the battle was ended. There was no gunfire behind him. He twisted and looked. Reg had the man whose horse had been dropped during the charge, upon his feet, unsteadily holding both arms aloft. The man had just let go a pistol.

Beyond, Dan Cowper was just arising from a prone body farther back, and two bewildered saddle-horses fully-rigged out, hovered back another dozen or two yards, watching.

Will arose, winced when his right hip pained him a little, walked over and started to toe over the man he had shot, but a sudden solid reverberation underfoot made him raise his head and watch five hard-riding horsemen making a grim race forward. He knew who the leader of those men was even at that distance, and turned back to examining the man at his feet.

'You got water?' husked the wounded man.

Will had no canteen but he looked over where the dying man's horse lay, then went after the canteen over there. He was hoisting the big man and trickling water into him when those horsemen slackened pace and walked their horses the last hundred yards, old George Hardin out front looking as forbidding as an ancient stone idol.

Will ignored the arrival of Ox-Yoke and concentrated upon helping the dying man. There was no doubt he would not linger long. Both Will's bullets had hit him high up. He was bleeding two ways, inwardly and outwardly.

Colonel Hardin alighted, stepped in for a closer look then shoved back his hat and sank to one knee. 'Ladd,' he said, ' you knew better than to come back here.'

This remark was the first evidence Will Chance had that the men he had fought were indeed the four renegades he had come up-country seeking. He'd never seen Ladd Denton up close before, either, and now he was propping him against a leg.

Denton gazed at old Hardin. 'I came back for you,' he said softly.

'For *her*,' corrected the colonel, and the outlaw's eyes flashed momentarily.

'The hell with her, you old bastard. I knew you kept money at the ranch.'

Colonel Hardin knelt in long silence gazing impassively at the dying outlaw, behind him Waite and the other Ox-Yoke men dismounted, finally, and walked on out where Dan Cowper and Reg Morgan were standing together. Off in the easterly distance a rider was coming head-on as fast as he could ride. That would be Herlihy; he would be chagrined from now until his final day that he had missed the fight.

Will watched Ladd Denton, thinking of all the exploits the notorious outlaw had lived through. And now he sat here dying in the middle of Ox-Yoke range, shot down by a cow-town constable.

Colonel Hardin said, 'Lay him back, Will.' The old Secesh officer had seen more than his share of this sort of departure. 'He's dead.'

It had been an easy passing for so famous a gunman, robber and killer. He had simply sighed, closed his heavy lids and Gone On.

Will arose to roll a smoke and look back where Herlihy was coming up and where the other men were glumly conversing. They had one survivor, the man whose horse had been shot out from under him in the first exchange.

Colonel Hardin waited until Will lighted his smoke before speaking. 'Son, you did right. We saw you charge them from where we cut north-easterly from the stage-road. You did it exactly right.'

Will ignored the compliment. 'You heard

what he said about Antonia?'

Hardin had. 'Yes, I heard.'

'Well; there's no sense in telling her, is there? If she loved him just the fact that he's dead'll be a hard enough blow for her.'

The older man's tough eyes softened. 'No sense at all. But maybe someday.'

'When we get back I'll turn her loose.'

Hardin nodded. 'All right.' He turned to look out where his riders were. 'We'll lend a hand rounding up their horses and helpin' you fellers get the bodies lashed down.'

Will was appreciative. 'I'm obliged, Colonel.'

Hardin shoved out a hand. They shook without speaking, but as the colonel started to turn away and lead his horse over where the others had congregated, he said, 'I didn't believe it'd end this way.'

Will looked around. 'Six hundred dollars worth of dead men, Colonel. For a lousy six hundred dollars . . . It's not worth it.'

Colonel Hardin stopped, turned and looked at the taller and younger man as he said, 'Son, it never is worth it. Never.'

We hope you have enjoyed this Large
Print book. Other Chivers Press or
Thorndike Press Large Print books are
available at your library or directly from the
publishers.

For more information about current and
forthcoming titles, please call or write,
without obligation, to:

Chivers Large Print
published by BBC Audiobooks Ltd
St James House, The Square
Lower Bristol Road
Bath BA2 3BH
UK
email: bbcaudiobooks@bbc.co.uk
www.bbcaudiobooks.co.uk

OR

Thorndike Press
295 Kennedy Memorial Drive
Waterville
Maine 04901
USA
www.gale.com/thorndike
www.gale.com/wheeler

All our Large Print titles are designed for
easy reading, and all our books are made to
last.